Nefarious Deeds

A Mel Addison Mystery Series

A NOVEL

BY

ANGELA ABDERHALDEN

Seventh Wave Books, LLC

NEFARIOUS DEEDS
A Mel Addison Mystery Series

Seventh Wave Books, LLC
2015

Seventh Wave Books, LLC
www.seventhwavebooks.com

First Paperback Edition: 2015

Nefarious Deeds is a novel by: Angela Abderhalden

ISBN-13: **978-1-938852-12-1** (pbk)

Cover design by Jason Wilcox

Printed in the United States of America

ANGELA ABDERHALDEN

Chapter 1

The achy feeling had been plaguing me for six months, rotating to different joints on different days. Today the joints in my knees had been hurting all day. As I twisted to place the employee file to the side on the finished pile, I got an achy feeling in my wrist. After setting the file down, I rubbed it. The aching was getting worse. For the last two days more than one joint had been hurting. *I should call Corbet's office again to see if they have the results of my tests yet.* With a sigh, I started on the next employee background check.

"Mel…" Pam appeared at my door.

I glanced up at the secretary with a smile. "Yeah?" *Anything would help to break up this boring day.*

"Uh, this lady on the phone has called four times today for Rich. And he still hasn't called in yet. She wants to talk to someone. I've left messages for Rich to call in, but so far nothing from him."

I frowned. "What is it about?"

Pam shook her head. "Rich took a new case several days ago but only spoke to John about it. I don't know what it concerns." She paused. "This lady sounds almost desperate. I can't reach John either. What should I do?"

I glanced at the blinking light of the phone. Even the blinking seemed impatient. "I'll talk to her. That's odd about Rich not telling us." I scrunched up my face in puzzlement at Pam who nodded in agreement. She left the doorway as I reached for the phone. "Hi. This is Mel. Can I help you?"

"Who is this?"

"Mel Addison. I'm a detective here. Rich has been busy all day. Can I help you, or can I relay a message to Rich for you?"

There was a pause on the line. "Are you related to Rich?"

"His little sister."

"Oh. Well…"

I waited. *Who is this lady?*

"I guess. I was wondering if they found out anything yet?"

I frowned. *This is odd. Rich working a case without me knowing anything about it.* Even though I was only the apprentice, it was unusual that I didn't at least have a passing knowledge of his case. "Not that I know of."

"Well, I hadn't heard from Palmer yet, so I decided to call Rich and ask."

"Palmer?"

"The private investigator I hired out here."

I cleared my throat of the phlegm that had gathered. "I've been out of the office for the past couple of days. Why don't you fill me in with the case, Mrs… I didn't catch you name?"

"Wanda. Wanda Zebring. Well, that's my maiden name. I'm currently switching it back to that from Carson." She paused.

I waited.

"My ex-husband kidnapped our daughter and the detective, Greg Palmer, I hired here in Trenton seems to think he might be there in Illinois."

I scrunched up my face, she had pronounced Illinois with the 's'. "Trenton? New Jersey?"

"Yeah. Palmer contacted Rich to see if your firm would investigate and find out. I haven't heard from anyone in two days. Carmine is…" The lady's voice broke.

"Ma'am?"

Wanda sniffled first. "Sorry. Carmine is my eight year old. She went missing six months ago. The police know Brady, my ex, took her. But… She's been through so much lately. See, Brady molested her last year."

I closed my eyes. I didn't want to hear anymore.

"I have sole custody of her, and Brady has a restraining order against him. But he is very possessive. He skipped bail and took her. Palmer thinks he's there. I was just wondering if Rich found anything, anything at all?"

I opened my eyes, tears swelling. I shook my head to compose myself. "I haven't heard anything from him. Let me do some checking with Rich, and I'll call you back. Give me a number I can reach you at this evening." I wrote down her phone number. "I promise, one way or the other Wanda, I will call you back."

"Thanks, Mel." Her voice sounded relieved. "I don't want to be a pest but the longer—"

"No, I understand Wanda." I smiled to inject it into my voice. "I do. I will call you."

"Thanks."

I hung up the phone and cursed softly. Standing up, I immediately went into his office and looked around on his desk. No file anywhere. I hesitated, then opened his file drawer. I knew I was snooping and shouldn't be in there, but this was important. Sure enough the file was there.

Brady Carson, according to the Private Investigative firm, Palmer Investigations, in New Jersey, molested and kidnapped his daughter from the custodial parent, Wanda Brady.

I looked at the picture of her in the file. She was a cute kid. Her picture showed a brown haired girl with glowing green eyes, and her smile was that of a fun loving child. Reaching out, I gently touched the girl's face. After several seconds I went back to reading the file.

All it said was that Brady had mentioned Quincy several times to Wanda's relatives in New Jersey. He seemed to be fascinated with my hometown and the surrounding area. Go figure.

Quincy, Illinois is a nice city. With about 45,000 people, it has the small town feel but with a bigger city shell. The town itself is not well known. Hannibal Missouri, famous for Mark Twain, is just fifteen minutes downstream on the Mississippi and better known. Still, for some reason, Brady had indicated he would return here.

Security Investigations is the only private investigative firm in Quincy. Rich and John Huddleston own it and took me on as an apprentice over a year ago. I still had two more years before I could legally call myself a detective.

I shook my head and sat down at Rich's desk. I closed the file, thinking about it. *Why didn't he tell me about this case?* The picture of the girl, which was sticking out of the top of the file, continued to draw my attention. I took it out again as tears swelled in my eyes.

I knew why Rich wasn't telling me. In my heart I did. He was trying to protect me, just like big brothers are supposed to do. Tucking the picture back into the file, I stuck it into his desk.

He really had no excuse though. I should've been informed. With a determined feeling settling into my bones, I headed back to my own office. I was going to find this girl and nail Brady's butt to the wall for his offenses. So help me God.

***

It was after six when I heard the door open. I stood up and waited in doorway. My office is directly across the hall from Rich's.

Rich glanced at me. "What are you still doing here?"

"Waiting for you."

Rich did a double take, then moved into his office with a puzzled look as he thumbed through a handful of call sheets from Pam's desk. "For?"

I followed him into his office and stood in front of the desk. "Wanda Carson called."

Rich flinched. He swallowed before looking up. "And?"

"Tell me why you kept information about this case from me." A noise caught my attention, and I swiveled my head to see John now standing in the doorway looking at us.

Rich glanced John's way too. Then his eyes came back to me. "I didn't want you involved."

"Why?"

"Robbie."

"That's not fair, Rich." My voice lowered. *So I had been right.* Rich was trying to spare me the pain of thinking about my dead son. Over a year and a half ago I had lost my husband and only son in a car accident.

"Maybe not, but I wanted to spare you the pain."

"So you kept it from me because you think I'm not strong enough?"

Rich sighed. "You're still too close to Robbie's death, Mel. I didn't want—"

"Maybe I could help!"

John stepped into the room. "Now that you know…" He glanced at Rich. "What do you want to do?"

My eyes caught John's. He was concerned too, I could tell. "I wanna help."

John looked at Rich.

I looked too. Rich's eyes finally met mine. Our blue eyes locked, then my big brother's eyes softened. "Okay, but I don't want you…"

The door opening in the front room caught all of our attentions. With a puzzled look, John headed out. Rich and I followed.

Standing inside the door, with a crooked smile, was an unexpected person.

Bart Hessor.

Chapter 2

Bart Hessor is known as the king pin of the drug dealers in Quincy. The police just haven't been able to pin anything on him. His aunt had been the head honcho before him but had been put in jail by my dad. I had had a brief relationship with Bart when we were teens during the blow up between his aunt and the law. Since returning to Quincy, Bart has renewed his interest in me, much to my chagrin.

I could feel Rich tense next to me. Both men glanced my way, and then Bart looked at me too. I cleared my throat. "Yes?"

"I want to hire you for a job," Bart said as he stuck his hands into the pockets of his light tan dress slacks. His professionally styled, blond hair was almost shiny in the light. "I need professional help tracking someone and…" Bart paused.

Rich and John exchanged looks. Again they looked at me.

"Don't look at me," I said softly. "I'm just a peon here." I smiled at my brother and he glared at me.

Rich turned his icy glare back to Bart. "No."

"Look, this is legit. I'm looking for—"

"No," Rich said with more conviction.

Bart's eyes narrowed. "Look, Rich. We've been at odds before. Be professional. I want to hire your firm. I'm willing to put aside the past because I need help. I'm not asking for your friendship or anything but your professional help. I've checked your firm out. You come highly recommended. Trust me, I didn't come here lightly."

Rich took a deep breath.

John glanced at me again, then glanced at Bart. "Sit. Tell us what you want, then we'll decided." He motioned to the chair in front of Pam's desk.

Bart hesitated then sat.

I watched as Rich glared at John then sat behind Pam's desk. John took a seat on the couch. I leaned on the hallway doorpost, arms crossed. This could not be good.

Bart glanced at me. He turned his attention back to my brother. "Here's the deal. I need to find out who my real parents are."

The silence in the room was deafening.

Bart looked at each of us before continuing. "Aunt Maddie won't tell me who my parents are, but I need to find out. Since I wasn't born here, there are no records. And I can't find any. My supposed birth certificate is fake. I checked it out. I'm clueless where to go next, that's why I'm here."

"Why do you need to know who your parents are?" Rich asked reluctantly.

Bart almost seemed embarrassed. He fiddled with his shirt for a second. "I've always wondered, and Aunt Maddie always refuses to tell me. I well, I've had some medical tests done and they turned out fine, but I'm curious about what other genetic issues I might need to know about."

Once more the silence was deep. I shifted on my feet as I watched Rich stare at his arch enemy. Rich, when he had been a police officer, had tried numerous times to catch Bart doing something—anything, illegal. Bart was crafty though and eluded him. No one on the police force could catch him doing anything more illegal than a parking violation. Rich got injured on the job and now Mitch, my other older brother, was currently trying to get Bart.

Rich knew that I hung around with Bart occasionally as teens but nothing more. Only John knew the depth of my previous relationship with Bart, and he had promised not to tell the family. A case several months ago had put me back in touch with Bart, and John had caught me on a date with Bart. I was using Bart to get information on a murder. Bart wanted to renew the relationship. I refused in no uncertain terms. Still he was persistent. No one in the family knew this. John was keeping silent about it for my sake. I had been rebellious in my youth, but time and age had mellowed me. I knew better than to start up again with Bart. So no matter what happened here, I was sure to be stuck in the middle.

Rich stood and looked at John. Their eyes locked for the briefest of seconds. "We need to talk about this."

Bart stood and met Rich's gaze. "Here's the rub. I need to hire you tonight, or I'm going with a firm in St. Louis. Not as good as you, and also without the local connections that I figure will be most important." He paused with a glance at me. "I realize that this is very uncomfortable for all of us. So here's my deal, then you can go discuss it. I'm willing to pay you twice your normal rate."

John stood with a suspicious look. "Why the rush and why twice?"

"Because I want to know for my peace of mind, and twice your normal amount because Rich and Mel know the behind the scenes situation. And I trust the firm's confidentiality. I don't want to air my dirty laundry to more people. And…" He smiled at Rich. "Believe it or not, I actually know you'll to do a good job."

"Sit," Rich ordered. "We'll be back." He motioned for me to move back to the conference room. John followed us.

Rich closed the door and glared at me.

"What did I do?" I asked innocently.

"Do you think he has ulterior motives?" Rich had his hands on his hips. His face was tight.

"What do you mean?"

"I just have a sneaking suspicion that he is here because of you." His blue eyes were hard.

I cursed, my legendary anger coming fast. I have a very short fuse. "I had nothing to do—"

John stepped between us. He first looked at me. "Calm." He then turned his gaze to Rich. "Don't be an ass, Rich. I know for a fact that Mel wants nothing to do with him."

Rich's eyes flicked to me then back to John. "And how do you know?"

John interrupted him. "Mel had some problems with him after, well, from before. I helped her make Bart understand that pursuing her would be wrong."

Rich looked down at the table. He took a deep breath. "So? What do you think, John?"

John crossed his arms in thought.

I shifted my weight. I knew that recently the guys had been having a very slow time finding cases. No cases meant no money. Money was tight. I had even offered at one point to stop working for them.

"I hate this," Rich said softly, then he cursed. His eyes met John's. "We need this."

John nodded reluctantly. "But with conditions."

Rich turned to me. "How about you? What do you think?"

"I have no say."

His eyes softened. "Yes, you do. You'll be the one to deal with his advances. If you don't want to do this, say so, and we'll refuse."

I glanced from Rich to John and back again. Both seemed willing to take my advice. I looked to the floor. When I looked up they were both still staring at me. I merely gave a nod.

Rich swore softly. "I hate this. Do you have any conditions in mind?" he asked John.

John nodded.

"I'll grab a contract," Rich said as he opened the door. "I hate this," was torn from him in a whisper.

John and I headed to the front entrance. Bart stood at our approach. His eyes met mine, and I refused to give any indication one way or the other.

"We'll take the case," John said. "But…"

Bart nodded for him to go on.

"There are conditions beyond the normal contractual conditions." John was staring Bart down now.

"I understand," Bart said as Rich joined us in the room, paper in hand.

"First of all, you work through me. No calls to Rich or Mel. I'm your contact. Second, if we find out that this is drug related, we end the contractual relationship immediately. You forfeit any and all monies, plus any that we have incurred."

I glanced to see Rich writing on the contract.

John continued, "Third, you will not come to the office again. I'll arrange to meet you somewhere else. I think you understand the reason."

"Sure."

"Lastly, you will leave Mel alone." John's voice turned hard.

Bart's eyes hardened too. He gave a passing glance at Rich who was watching him, then his eyes turned to mine. They narrowed slightly. After several seconds he returned his eyes to John. "Done."

John nodded. "Rich."

Rich quickly went through the usual explanation of the form for Bart. It was signed, including initialing the added clauses. Bart handed a check to Rich.

John spoke up. "Tomorrow I'll call you and we'll meet. At that time I'll get all the information about what you need. Agreed?"

"Agreed." Bart hesitated then left the office.

I let out my breath. The air seemed to expand from it's condensed state, which it had been in since Bart entered.

Rich leaned back in the chair. "I hate this." He shook his head and stood up, heading back to his office with contract and check.

John turned to me lowering his voice. "Any outside contact with Hessor, I mean any, and you call me."

I nodded.

"I'm serious."

"I know. Trust me, I don't want him around." I said sticking my hands in my pockets.

"If he finds out that you're hurting, he may try and exploit that."

"Hurting?" I asked glancing up.

"About Max."

I could feel my mouth tightening, and I opened it to spew venom at John.

John took one step towards me and touched my lips with his finger. He'd used this tactic to disarm me before. "I know you've been tracking Bauer. And I know that it's not sitting well with you. Rebounding is a dangerous time."

Rich appeared at the doorway. A puzzled look flashed on his face.

John moved away from me with a glance at Rich.

"What's going on?" Rich asked.

"I'm just warning Mel about Hessor."

"John's being a total jerk, is what. I'm calling Wanda back, then I'm out of here."

***

I was sitting in Dad's bar sipping a beer later that night. I felt like crap, again. I was tired and achy. And I felt another cold coming on. I hadn't been able to shake this cold thing for about the last six months.

The bar was quiet tonight. Dad was gossiping at the other end of the bar with an old friend. I was nursing my beer.

A body slid in next to me. "Hey, WT."

I grunted at Mitch.

"Such a sunny disposition." He smiled then shook his head at Dad and the offer of a beer.

"Yeah."

Mitch glanced around. There was no one near us. "Talk to me."

I turned to him.

"Something has been eating at you for a while—since you came back from California, six months ago."

I turned back to staring at the beer bottle. I didn't like to talk about things like this, and Mitch knew it too. That was probably why it had taken him this long to talk to me.

"It's about Max, isn't it?"

I didn't respond.

"What happened in California between the two of you? Besides the shooting." Mitch grabbed my beer and took a swig of it.

"Get your own beer, turd head." I grabbed it back.

"That's the feisty sister I'm used to." Mitch grinned.

I glanced around. "I slept with him."

"Good."

My eyes fell back on my brother. Mitch and I have always been close. Being only a year or so a part age-wise, we had hung out together in high school. I had dated his friends and he dated mine. Of the family members, Mitch understands me best.

"I think it was good for you," Mitch said taking another drink of my beer. "It was about time."

"Yeah." It had been one year, to the day, from the car accident the night I slept with Max.

I had met Max on my first case with Rich and John, on my return to Quincy from Maryland after the accident. Max had been a police Detective here in town, and we had clashed over territory on a murder case. Despite that, we had become friends. More, he had wanted to date me, but I knew I wasn't ready yet. He left to return to California and a new job. We kept in touch, and when a case took us to California, I spent the night with him. It was then that he expressed his true feelings for me. He told me he loved me, had from the first we met.

I left him on the spot. I ran. Soon after coming to my senses, I tried to contact him, but he wasn't answering my calls. And he had quit the force in California. Then I tracked him just like John said. I tracked him to Texas. Last month, I had stopped tracking him. He wanted nothing to do with me.

"What happened with Max, WT?"

WT was a nickname Mitch had given me in our youth. He was one of the few who still called me that. It was after the song, *Wild Thing* by The Troggs.

"Nothing."

"Liar."

I sighed. "As you said a long time ago, he fell hard for me."

"And he told you so," Mitch said quietly.

I nodded.

"You ran."

I nodded again.

"Now you want him back."

I snorted.

Mitch chuckled. "Don't take that tone with me. You miss him."

12

"I miss his friendship. Nothing more." I finished the bottle.

"Sure." Mitch motioned to our dad, who slid another beer down the bar. Mitch caught it and handed it to me. "Where is Max?"

"I don't know."

"Sure."

"No, really. I tracked him for a while, but he refused my calls." I shrugged as I took a drink. "I'm better off any way."

"Not true. Besides, Max is a much better guy than Craig. Any day." Mitch smiled. We sat there for some time not saying anything. "Larry, Kick and me are hitting the river this weekend. Wanna come?"

I shrugged. "Wait and see. I might be coming down with something."

Mitch's face turned concerned. "You just got over a cold. Maybe you ought to see a doctor."

"I have. Just a cold."

Mitch reached for my beer again.

I moved it out of his reach.

His left hand began tickling me. I squirmed but kept the beer away from him. He kept tickling me until he could grab the beer.

"I hope you get my cold." I smirked as he guzzled from the bottle.

Mitch laughed as he stood. Handing the beer back, he said, "Let me know about the skiing."

"Yeah." I watched as Mitch left the bar. Soon I was heading home too. I was dead dog tired.

Chapter 3

John sat at the conference room table with a file the next day. We were eating Maid Rites, a delectable local sandwich, and the smell was glorious. He had just come from his meeting with Hessor. "It looks pretty upfront."

Rich had an almost permanent scowl on his face. "Yeah?" If he chewed much harder, I was afraid he might break a tooth.

John slid the file to him. "Hessor gave me copies of his fake birth certificate and everything else he found out about his birth, which is very little. He suggested we try finding his old nanny. He has had no luck locating her himself."

"Who?"

"He remembers her as only Anna, but he found some old employee records of his aunt's that list her as Ava Papios. Copies of the records are in the file. She was his nanny until he was around five. After he went to school, he doesn't remember her any more. My guess is that Madeline Hessor got rid of her because she was no longer needed."

Rich paged through the file. "There's not much here."

John nodded in agreement.

"Why won't Madeline tell Bart who his parents are?" I asked as I popped a cheddar crisp in my mouth; there's nothing better than deep-fried cheese.

John shrugged. "Hessor doesn't understand it either. He said he's asked numerous times on visits to her in prison, besides asking as a kid. She refuses to talk about it."

I frowned. It seemed a stupid thing to keep secret, if you asked me. "Maybe she kidnapped him or it was drug related."

"With Madeline Hessor you can almost count on it," Rich said still looking at the paperwork. "So, Ava Papios is the only lead."

"Right now," John said. "I'm sill checking on the city in Georgia where he's listed as being born. We should plan on checking into kidnapped babies or missing children at the time. To be honest, I'm very skeptical. I think the birth certificate is fake. I think he was born elsewhere."

I rubbed my chin in thought. With a quick move I reached for the phone. It took a few seconds, but it was finally answered.

"Reference desk."

"Hi Judy, it's Mel. I need a favor, when you get time."

"Sure. What can I do for you?" Judy was a librarian that I'd gone to school with. She worked the reference desk at the local library.

I saw that both guys were now staring at me. I smiled. "I need you to do some foot work for me through the old files when you have time. You'll probably have to delve into old microfiche files even, old newspapers and such."

"Wait a minute, let me write this down." I heard her pushing papers around. "Go ahead."

"I need anything connected to the Hessor family from…" I hesitated and motioned for the file from Rich. I quickly paged through to find Bart's birth date, which I gave to Judy.

"Okay, until when?"

"Summer 1983 and Madeline's arrest for dealing drugs."

"That will take awhile."

"No problem. When you finish just let me know. I'll reward you the regular way."

Judy chuckled and we said our goodbyes.

"The regular way?" Rich asked amused.

"I take her out for lunch and ice cream."

Both men chuckled. John asked, "What are you looking for?"

I shrugged. "Nothing in particular, but any scandals should show up in the paper. It might give us other names."

Rich nodded. "In the meantime, run Ava Papios's name through the usual files. Do Bart's and Madeline's too, just to cover our bases. And check into missing kids in Georgia around his birth too." He paused. "Can you think of anything else John?"

John shook his head as he glanced at his watch. "I need to be heading out. See if I can't catch that bail skip for A1 Bail Bonds."

Rich stood up and handed the file to me. "Did you get those employee checks done, Mel?"

"On your desk next to your phone. Didn't you see them?"

"I was busy. Thanks."

We all headed back to our offices with John leaving shortly.

"Hey Rich?"

"Yeah?" He called back across the hallway.

I scooted out of my desk and headed to his office. "I was thinking last night…"

"This has got to be good," Rich said with a smile.

I smirked. "Why is Brady Carson so enamored with Quincy?"

Rich shrugged. "All I could find out was that he was arrested on a drunk and disorderly charge while he lived here. Other than that, he appeared to have lived a normal life. As far as I could find, he lived in the Quincy area only about two years before moving to New Jersey where he met Wanda and they got married. Why?"

I frowned. "What's here that would be so great? Does he have family here?"

Rich shook his head. "Family lives in Florida. A suburb of Jacksonville."

"Then what?"

Another shrug.

I considered everything that Quincy had to offer. For the locals it was a lot, but what might bring someone to town? I couldn't think of anything. "Where did he live when he was here?"

Rich grabbed the file on the corner of his desk. He paged through it. "For a time, on eighth street near Cedar. Then for a while on the outskirts of town on the Crabtree farm. He rented it from Isabella Crabtree."

"A farm?" That sounded weird. *Why would a person who was not a farmer rent a farm?* A sudden thought struck me. "Did Brady hunt?"

Rich's eyes took on a surprised look. "A hunter? Good idea, Mel. Yeah. Possible. Very possible." He nodded. "I wonder if the state has records from back then?"

I watched as Rich ran the information through his brain. Finally he looked up at me.

"Really good, Mel. I knew there was a reason we kept you on board." His tone was joking. "I'll look into it. I know someone in the Department of Natural Resources that I can sweet talk into verifying it for me. Thanks."

I chuckled and headed back to my office and the computer. All I had to do today was computer work on Bart's case. After that, I was dead in the water for things to do.

***

"Okay Mel, what have you found out?" Rich asked the next morning at our daily meeting.

I opened the file. "With Bart's birth certificate, I found that, as John said, the doctor doesn't exist. According to birth records at the hospital, there were no baby boys born that day. Along with that, missing children records are sketchy during those days, but I found no indication that there were any missing babies in that area. I even widened the search for the whole state of Georgia during that week. Only one child went missing, a girl, and she turned up dead a year later. Death listed as respiratory illness, no charges filed on the parents, even though they hid the death.

"On the subject of Ava Papios, she lived here in town during Bart's younger days as he said. She worked as his nanny. When he turned five and went to school, she left Quincy and moved to St. Louis. She worked for Griffin Industries for about three years. It dead ends there."

"Where did she go?" John asked leaned back relaxed.

I shrugged. "I can't find her anywhere. According to all the records I searched, she has never held another job since then. No income. No

17

health records. No nothing. According to the data files, she disappeared."

"What did she do at this Griffin Industries?" Rich asked. He leaned up on his elbows.

"I couldn't get a firm answer. I even tried calling the business to find out about her position. I got stonewalled. They have the records, but no one I spoke to had access to them. The one person who could bring something up on the computer said it shows that she worked in Human Resources. I'm guessing, but I'd have to say maybe a secretary."

John looked off to the side of the room deep in thought.

"Hmmm." Was Rich's comment. "Any other names or anything?"

I shook my head.

"What about scandals with Madeline?" Rich asked.

"Judy got me some information from around Bart's birth. It seems that several months after Bart was born, Madeline's husband Horace was killed in a Breaking and Entering. He was found dead in the study."

"How?" John asked me.

"His head was bashed in," Rich answered. "I remember Dad talking about it years later. Dad was a patrolman then, I think. Horace was found with his head caved in. Nothing was taken if I recall. I think Madeline found him…" Rich seemed to be looking off into space. "When she returned from somewhere. I can't remember where now. I'm pretty sure that the case was left unsolved."

"It's listed as a botched robbery in the papers," I reported, hefting the copy of the article.

Rich nodded. "But officially I think it's still open. Too many unanswered questions."

"Was Bart in the house by this time?" John asked. "Do we know when he came to live with his aunt?"

Both of us shook our heads.

"I'll ask him," John said. "I'll check with some contacts in St. Louis to see if I can't find out more about Griffin Industries. They make plastics, I'm pretty sure. Maybe I can get a peek in their personnel files to search more." He paused. "Where do we stand on the kidnapping case?"

Rich sighed. "Same as before. Nowhere."

I narrowed my eyes at my brother. "But?"

Rich glanced at John first. "My experience in cases like this would tend to indicate that the girl is probably dead."

I sucked in a silent breath.

"Here or there?" John asked.

Rich shrugged. "I've been talking with the neighbors around the farm. They seem to think that there is someone staying on the property, maybe. A guy. But no girl. I hate to say this, but I think the girl is dead and maybe buried on the property." Rich glanced at me.

"Have you talked to the owner of the farm?"

Rich shook his head. "I can't reach her. I hear she has become a recluse. Mrs. Crabtree won't answer or return my calls. She's renting the property to a Trisha Bashington. Trisha pretty much won't speak to me either. I'm not sure why." Rich paused. "Mel, you wanted to help? Go talk to the Trisha. Maybe being a woman, she might respond to you."

"I'll try." I scratched my arm. "If Crabtree is a recluse, who's looking after the property?"

Rich read the file on the table. "Uh, Ralph Zimmerman."

"Ralphie Zimmerman?" I asked surprised.

"Do you know him?" John asked.

I nodded. "I used to work with him at Kmart in the lawn department."

"Good." Rich smiled. "Talk to him. See if you can find out anything. Ask if we can search the wooded property. Come to think of it, ask if we can search the whole property."

"Why search?"

Rich almost grimaced. "I want to see if there are any fresh diggings."

"You can't just assume that Carmine is dead, Rich."

"Statistics would lean toward—"

I made a face at him as I interrupted. "We're talking about her life. I don't think we should be writing her off yet."

"I agree. That's why we're still looking. We aren't even getting that much money from this case," Rich said gently. "But you have to face facts."

I only gave him a slight nod. I didn't have to face facts, and I certainly didn't have to agree with them. I wasn't going to give up until there was a body found.

Chapter 4

"I haven't seen anyone like that."

I sighed. "Look, I work for a private detective agency in Quincy. I just need to know if you've seen any man with a girl on the property. Maybe hunting off season or just any suspicious movement in the woods." I swung my hand to indicate the wooded area only a hundred yards from the house.

The house had seen better days. It was a typical two story farmhouse—white with a small porch out front and a screened-in bigger porch on the back, built like a tall rectangle. The road was dirt as was the area where her car was parked. Weeds grew up farther away from the house with only a small half acre area that was kept cut. Several hundred yards away was an old decrepit barn that was beginning to fall down. It had at one time been a useful structure but now was in disrepair and disuse. Its two big wooden doors faced the dirt road. A metal and brick silo stood off to the right side of the barn. It too was no longer used. The top had long ago fallen in. Of the two, it looked the more sturdy.

The twenty year old woman shook her brown haired head as she rubbed her arm. Then she shoved her hands into the pockets of her jeans. She shifted on her feet. "Not around here, but I don't go in the woods often."

"How about as you drive in or out?"

Another shake of her head, causing her long pony tail to swing in the opposite direction.

I glanced around. It was quiet here. I almost sighed. As I turned around, I noticed her staring intently at me. "Okay, here's my card in case you see anyone. I would appreciate a call if you do."

Reluctantly she reached out and took it.

"How big is this farm? Do you know?"

The lady shrugged. "I think the guy said something like 200 acres or something. Mostly wooded. There are some old fields that are no longer used on the other side, I think. Why?"

"Well…" I smiled. "My brothers and I like to hunt. This looks like a really cool place, and it probably doesn't get a lot of use from other hunters. But with the other farms in the area, I bet it holds at least one trophy buck."

Trisha nodded. "So I've been told. A, uh, friend told me this was a little hidden gold mine for hunting."

"Is it actively hunted by anyone?" I swung my glance around the area again as though I was actually considering it.

"Not that I know of." She shifted her weight again and once more began rubbing her arm.

"Hmmm. Maybe I'll tell Mitch about it and see if we can get permission to hunt here this fall." I turned back to her with a smile. "Thanks." I shook her hand.

As I left, I noticed that she watched me until I had driven around a bend in the road and was obscured by the trees. I made a mental note to find a plan of the property so I could get the actual dimensions.

***

"Mel…" John said the next day as he passed my office. With a hand flick, he motioned for me to follow. Rich was already moving toward John's office.

After we were seated, John smiled at us. "We got a break on the Hessor case. Maybe."

Rich nodded for him to go on.

"Last night I drove to St. Louis to meet with several contacts. We struck pay dirt on one. Ava Papios did work for Griffin Industries. She was a secretary as you suspected Mel. And, it turns out that Griffin

Industries gives regularly to several charities in the area. I spoke with several older employees who used to work with her. They're having a get together at a charity fundraiser this weekend, during and after the party. Griffin Industries, along with several other businesses, are giving money to the charity for sick kids. By luck, a Mrs. Grasicolli, who is part owner of Griffin, will be there giving money from the business and a foundation she runs, to the charity. The fundraiser is partly to get money and partly to publically thank Mrs. Grasicolli."

"Yeah, so?" I asked.

"Hessor is also involved with this charity. I spoke with him early this morning. He knew all about the fundraiser." John paused. "It's a long shot, but a source said that she might be there. Apparently a bunch of the old employees are getting together that weekend and she has been invited. Although no one could identify who invited her. I'm still working on that. Anyway, the retirement fund of Griffin's is paying for seating for the retired employees or something. Hessor thought it might be a good idea to attend the fundraiser. Not only to see if she shows up but also to speak with Mrs. Grasicolli. Maybe she knows of Ms. Papios, very doubtful but we can ask, or at least it might give us better access to the business files."

Rich looked thoughtful. "That's an awfully big long shot."

John nodded in agreement. "True."

"We don't even know what this lady looks like." I threw in my two cents.

John shook his head and tossed an envelop onto the table. "Hessor dug up several old pictures of himself and Papios. He had her face computer aged. One is aged to when she worked at Griffin Industries; the other is what she might look like now."

Rich was already in the envelope, then handed them to me. "Still a long shot."

"The longest." John agreed. "But Hessor wants us to go. He's 'paying' the seating fee for us to be there."

"How much a plate?" Rich asked.

"One hundred and fifty."

Rich whistled then grimaced. "Let me guess, he wants Mel to go as his date."

John nodded. "I told him that was up to Mel. Either way, I explained to him that I was also going. He agreed."

Rich turned to me. "Mel?"

"A fundraiser? I hate those things." I made faces at the guys. I really did hate those sort of parties. Craig and I had to attend many of them with his law firm. "I don't have an appropriate dress. I got rid of all of them when I moved back here."

John sort of smiled. "Hessor must have guessed that. He has an account at the Bon. He said he'd call today and let them know to let you charge to him. And you get to keep the dress."

I cursed softly.

Rich started laughing. "Last time I saw Mel in a dress was at her wedding."

"Is this that important, John?" I asked.

"Could be. Could be a waste of time."

I grimaced. "I'll do whatever you guys think is best, but just know I hate formal dresses."

Rich turned to John. "I agree it's a long shot, but right now it's all we have, plus it's billable hours to Hessor. Just keep an eye on him. I don't trust him farther than I can spit."

John nodded in agreement. "I'll be with her the entire time." He turned to me. "Can you be ready by Thursday afternoon? That gives you two days."

"Yeah," I said reluctantly.

"Teresa's in town, Mel. Take her with you," Rich said.

"Yeah, if anyone would be able to get me into the right kind of dress, it'll be Teresa," I said. Teresa was my older sister, and she knew all about fashion. I, on the other hand, was clueless.

***

I walked into the office Thursday at four wearing the dress. It was a black dress from some big name designer, and cost a mint. Teresa splurged since Bart was footing the bill. After what seemed like hours of trying on dresses, Teresa finally settled on a formal one. She picked out a long black flowing gown that hit me just at the top of my shoes, which would give a hint of my black shiny pumps, also picked out by Teresa. She loved the way the slinky material clung in all the right places.

The back dropped low, a bit too far for my comfort, and the front had a shallow plunging neckline. I thought showing to my sternum was a bit extreme, but Teresa assured me that it was just right. She was having a ball accessorizing me too. She picked out a pair of conservative gold dangle earrings and a diamond-cut gold cuff that cost more than one of my paychecks. I found a necklace that I liked, but Teresa said not to wear it since it would take away from wow factor of the dress. I bought it anyway. Teresa even came over and dressed me this afternoon, chatting excitedly about the black tie event while fixing my hair. She pulled the front up and left the back loose. This past six months I had let it grow longer, and Teresa said it was just the right length to pull this off. I was glad to get away from Ms. Fashionista, but I still found myself smiling at the afternoon playing dress-up with Teresa.

Pam gasped and her eyes almost bugged out of her head. "Wow, Mel. You look great."

I looked down at myself and smoothed the dress. "Really?"

"Oh my, yes."

"I feel so uncomfortable."

"But you look fabulous."

I shrugged. "Is John here yet?" He and I were driving together in his car. The only thing I had left to do was put on the God-forsaken, matching black shiny heels. These I carried in my hand. I had tennis shoes on right now.

"No. He called a few minutes ago, said he was running late. Something about his tux."

I hesitated with a smile. "I bet he looks good in a tux."

Pam chuckled with a nod.

"Mel?" Rich called down the hall.

"Yeah?" I headed to his office. As I stopped in the doorway, he barely glanced up but did look at my feet.

He started chuckling. "I like the shoes. It reminds me of your prom."

I smiled. The group of girls I hung around with wore tennis shoes to the prom our senior year. Nice dressy tennis shoes but not heels. We were the hit and talk of the prom that year. "Yeah."

He nodded in approval anyway, then went back to his paperwork.

"Teresa did a good job picking out the dress, I guess." I brushed at the dress again. "Did John say anything about how long this thing would last?"

"The charity thing itself until after midnight, but from his sources, Mrs. Grasicolli wasn't staying long after the meal."

I nodded in response, then I sneezed.

"Another cold?" Rich asked without looking up.

"Yeah."

The door opened, and I glanced down the hall. John had just walked in dressed in everything but the jacket. The white shirt and black bowtie, along with his black vest, emphasized his upper body. *If he looks this good in a tux, I wonder what he looked like in dress uniform?*

John's eyes met mine, then traced my body. He quickly moved down the hall. "Mel… You look… Uh, great. Beautiful."

"But? Did I miss something?" I looked myself over, touching my dress near my breasts. *Are my boobs showing?*

John was still looking at me. "That is way too enticing a dress."

"What? What do you mean?" I brushed at the dress again.

John sighed. "You probably don't have any other dress do you?"

I shook my head.

He took a deep breath. "Okay, just watch yourself around Hessor." John's eyes panned me again, almost involuntarily.

I turned to see Rich looking me up and down. He seemed to be looking at me, not as a brother but as a man. "Oh my God! You're right, John. Mel what were you thinking?"

"What? I didn't even pick this out. Teresa did."

Rich and John's eyes met.

"It's too late now."

Rich cursed. "John, you watch out for her. Maybe I should go too."

"Rich, I can watch out for myself. Are we leaving anytime soon John? The sooner we do this, the sooner I can get this high-priced black handkerchief off me."

26

John chuckled as he slightly bowed and motioned for me to go ahead of him. "Ma'am."

I shook my head and headed out. Within minutes we were on the road to St. Louis.

***

We met Bart at the convention center where the fundraiser was being held. It was a huge building, but he was in the entrance waiting for us as planned. He looked nice in his suit with tie, but not as nice as John. His tuxedo jacket finished off his attire just right.

Bart's eyes not only panned up and down me, but they got wider. Bart sort of licked his lips. John took the valet ticket and held out his elbow to escort me to the door. As we entered, John's phone rang. He pulled it out of his pocket as Bart walked toward us.

"Gotta take this. Watch Hessor."

John met Bart's eyes in what looked like a sort of warning, then excused himself and moved off to the side to answer his phone.

Bart's eyes traced up and down my body. When they finally met mine, it looked like he was having a hard time controlling himself.

"Don't even. I do not want to date you, so just perish the thought from your mind."

Bart took me by the arm and moved over to the wall. He leaned me against it, then placed his hands on either side of me. He leaned in close and whispered in my face, "Mel, I'm gonna do you some day. Not today and maybe not tomorrow. But someday. And it'll be the best you have ever had. I promise. If I hadn't made the deal with your brother and Huddleston, I'd do you right now. But soon, Mel. The best you've ever had." He pushed off the wall, adjusted his suit coat, then looked at me. The intent was obvious.

I swallowed the big lump in my throat. *Crap. I don't need this.*

***

The longer I mingled, the more I remembered how much I hated these formal affairs. This had been one of Craig and my many arguments. As his practice had taken off, I was required to attend more and more formal affairs. Not that they were particularly bad, just boring. The people were usually snooty and stuck on themselves.

The room had tables near a platform at one end. The area I was in now was open, almost like a dance floor, where people were gathering. Along the back wall were two bars, staffed and serving drinks to those that didn't want the wine being handed out.

I tugged at the waist part of my dress as I checked out an older lady across the room. I caught John's eye and nodded with my head. He had just finished talking with an older gentleman. His eyes panned to the lady and he shook his head. We were trying to speak to the older people there to possibly get a clue about Papios.

I glanced down and wondered, for about the hundredth time, if my boobs were falling out. Not that I'm very big in the chest, but it felt like I was getting no support there. The two strips of thin, black, shear material seemed to barely cover me up. The only good thing about this dress was that it would soon be coming off. And the pumps. The longer I wore them, the more I remembered swearing off them.

Okay, time to do my thing. I headed over to the group with the older lady. The younger man and his girlfriend moved on, and I slid up next to the older woman of about sixty. "Hi. Enjoying the event?"

"Of course. My Edward is on the board here. I love the party atmosphere. Don't you?"

"Absolutely. And it's all for a good cause too."

"Cause? Oh yes, the sick kids." She giggled as she swapped her drink for another from the roving waiter. If I were a bartender, I might be thinking of cutting her off.

"Do you work?" I was holding onto my glass that I had dumped into an empty glass on a nearby table an hour ago.

Another giggle. "You are funny. Dear Edward makes more money than…." She prattled on for sometime about her husband and his financial genius. She wasn't Papios and wouldn't have had a clue. As soon as I could, I politely left her side.

I smiled a nice, friendly 'get away from me' smile at another high society lady that I had already spoken to earlier as I slowly made my way around the room. My eyes took in the people standing around gossiping and talking about what their dogs ate for lunch or something just as stupid. I would much rather be sitting at Dad's bar talking shop with the guys. Still, Bart was paying us a great deal of money.

I looked around to find John, but he was nowhere in sight. Black and white tuxes all around made it hard to actually find him. Or Bart. Not that I particularly wanted to be by Bart, but I at least wanted to know where he was. I didn't want to be surprised by him.

I took a long look at a lady that might resemble the lady we were looking for. I headed toward her, but when I got close, her accent placed her from Russia or somewhere similar. *Nope. I wish this was over.* I handed my long empty glass to a waiter as he walked by and flexed my foot. My ankles and knees ached today. *I need a beer.*

Slowly I made my way over to the bar. At least the rich and mighty knew how to drink. I was allowing myself one beer now and one after the meal, if it could be called a meal. It was probably one of those meals where the food is the size of a half dollar and tastes like it's made out of cardboard. I sighed again but kept the smile on my face. I knew how to play this game, as much as I hated it. I had learned how from the wife of an old Judge back in Maryland. She had been a hoot and hated going to formal affairs too. I shook myself. I hated those nights. Those wasted nights schmoozing for the law firm.

With a quick nod to the bartender, I got his attention. He moved down the small bar with the obligatory smile.

"Yes, Ma'am?"

"Please tell me you have beer, Jeremy." I smiled at him after reading his name tag, but my eyes were actually pleading with him.

A large, genuine smile lit his face. "But of course. I take it you're not a wine person?"

"Not hardly." This was my kind of person. "I even tend bar on the side." I winked. "Do you make much money with this gig?"

"Some days." He glanced down the bar, but seemed to be content to let the others work those who had just moved up to the bar. Apparently I wasn't the only one not wanting wine. It wasn't shoulder to shoulder but more people seemed to be gathering at the bar. "Tonight is a so, so night. What's your choice?"

"Do you have local micro brews?"

"Two."

"Pick the smoothest one and sock it to me."

"Coming up." He quickly moved to the back side of the bar and dug in a case. Shortly, he returned to the bar, pouring from a bottle into a chilled glass. He handed it over. "Smooth and tasty."

With a big smile I tried a drink. "Hmmm… Good. Thanks." I placed several bills in his tip jar. "I'll be back later. Save me another of these, if you would."

He blasted me with a huge smile. "Yes, ma'am." Jeremy glanced past me to the next customer.

I started to back away. As I did, I accidently bumped into a man dressed in one of the rarer white tux jackets. I turned as I managed to not spill my beer. I gave a slight cough that had been threatening all night. "Sorry." I managed to get out around the cough.

The man was staring at me.

I glanced up to look at his face to see who this rude man was.

Max Bauer.

Chapter 5

He had changed a lot since I last saw him. Max was now wearing his hair longer. It touched the bottom of his ears and the front was feathered back in a natural way. He had grown a beard and mustache, both well-trimmed and very sexy looking.

I looked him up and down involuntarily. He had gotten even more trim. The bright white jacket and shirt were off set by a deep black bow tie. And the cut of the tux was tailored to show off his body. He looked like a million dollars. Yummy. Handsome cake, and I could feel myself almost drooling.

Max was giving me the eye too. I saw his eyes roaming me as I had done him. His eyes finally met mine, and they were cold and deep dark blue. Yet for just a second I had noticed a different look in them. Now it was gone. And his face was set; there was no smile in it.

"Max?"

"Hello, Mel." He turned to the bartender and ordered a scotch and water, then his attention was back. "What are you doing here?" But it didn't sound like he cared.

"Uh…you look great. What have you been doing lately?" My heart was beating faster than normal. I took a shallow but hopefully, calming breath. I glanced down and noticed that my hand was shaking. I stopped my eyes from wandering over him again.

"This and that." He stuck one hand in a pocket, the other he placed on the bar. Max seemed to be deciding what to do; his expression was flickering between curiosity and feigned indifference.

"I tried calling several times. You either didn't answer or something. Then you moved." I took a drink of my beer for lack of something better to do with my hands.

Max nodded. "I quit the force. I moved on." He thanked Jeremy and left him a tip, then turned back to me. He was casually holding the glass in his hand, giving it a slight swirl every now and then.

"Yes, I know. I spoke to Detective Lexon. Where did you go after you moved to Texas?"

"You knew I moved to Texas?"

"It's what I do, track people. Since you wouldn't return my calls, I stopped tracking you." I swallowed again, my heart was still beating too fast, but at least my hands were no longer shaking. I took another sip of the beer. "So, where do you live now?"

Max shrugged. "Around."

"Doing?"

"Why?"

I sighed. "Fine. If that's how you want to play this." I made a movement to go but was stopped by his hand on my arm.

"Why are you here?"

"I'm looking for someone."

Max hesitated at that, and his hand dropped from my arm. "A case? Still working for Rich and John?"

I nodded. "We're searching for someone. Rumor has it that she might show up or at least someone that knows her might show up." I looked around. "Otherwise, I wouldn't be here. I had enough of this kind of crap with Craig."

Max almost smiled. He shook his head. Finally his eyes betrayed him. "You look nice. How are the ribs?"

"Fully healed. Physical therapy helped a lot." I took another drink and looked around. "What are you doing here?"

"My Grandmother."

"Excuse me?"

"My Grandma forced me to be here. She's giving away a bunch of money and wanted someone from the family with her. Mom and Dad are in Europe again. So, I got stuck." Max shrugged.

I felt my jaw drop slightly. "Your Grandmother is Mrs. Grasicolli?"

Max nodded with amusement in his eyes. "Yeah. Mom's mom."

I gathered my wits. I knew from my time in California that his family was rich, but not this rich. It was said that she and her family were one of the richest families in the country. They gave away more money than some countries made in a year. I smiled. "So, that's why your mom didn't like your 'job'?"

Max nodded taking a big drink from his glass.

"What do you do now?"

"Anything I want," Max said glancing up to the platform at the front of the room. "Grandma came out to California after you left and talked me into traveling with her. I'm sort of her gofer."

"But—"

"So here's where you've been." A man's voice spoke over my shoulder.

I first noticed Max's reaction. He looked up in surprise at the voice, as though he had been totally absorbed in me. Then his face turned to stone, his eyes ice cold blue. His eye narrowed as he looked at me.

I almost flinched. Bart was standing behind me.

"Well, well, well. If it isn't one of the nation's finest." Hessor stepped up next to me. His shoulder was almost touching mine. "Bauer, right?" He held out his hand.

Max looked at it. He looked back at Bart and nonchalantly took a drink of his glass.

Hessor smiled and dropped his hand. He turned to me. "Mel, we need to be heading to the table. It's about time for this thing to start." He offered me his arm with a smirk at Bauer.

Max's eyes hardened even more as he looked at me.

I could tell what he was thinking. He felt betrayed. I could see it in his eyes. "Max, it's not what you think…"

Bart took me by the arm and started to lead me toward the tables. "I want you to meet someone…"

I looked back at Max, and he was following us with his eyes. He leaned on the bar and gulped down the rest of his drink. I watched as he set the glass on the bar and shook his head at Jeremy.

Our eyes met. Max stared with an icy blue look. The room actually turned colder. His face was set in stone. Then he turned and walked away.

I cursed under my breath. I wanted to go after him and explain why I was here with Hessor. But he disappeared into the crowd and Bart still had a hold of my arm. I removed my arm from his hand and while still trying to find Max in the crowd, nodded at the people he was talking to.

Max vanished into the crowd. You would think being one of the few white tuxes, he would be easy to spot, but no. I cursed at Bart silently but made nice to the people we were standing with. I now actually looked at them. They looked more uncomfortable than I did.

"We're so honored to be here. And thanks again for your help, Mr. Hessor," the man was saying. He tugged at his collar a bit trying to make the necktie not seem so much like a noose. From the look of his hands, he probably worked with them for a living and rarely wore suits.

I smiled at him and his wife. She too seemed to be on edge. I quickly thought back to the start of this conversation when I had been only half listening, trying to find Max in the crowd. *What are their names? Uh, Taylor... no, Tislor... no, Taymor?*

"I'm just happy we could help Jimmy out, Mr. Taylor," Bart said looking behind the man. "That's what this charity is about, helping kids. I think his speech will thrill Mrs. Grasicolli. She has always contributed, but this year we have her here with us."

Jimmy was scared. I could tell. He had on a cute little suit but was constantly pulling at his tie too. Due to his leukemia, he was bald, but on him it looked adorable. He stood behind his dad holding onto his leg, peeking at us.

I caught his eye and smiled.

Jimmy smiled back, a shy and scared smile.

"How old are you, Jimmy?" I asked as we moved to the round table near the front.

Bart was one of the local big wigs who supported this charity. He apparently gave a good deal of money to the St. Louis foundation. I'm sure not many people realized where the money came from though. Still, he was doing some good with it.

"He's six. Normally, he's not this shy," Mr. Taylor answered for his son, then pried the boy from his legs. "Come on Jimmy. What's the problem, son?"

Jimmy didn't say anything but shook his head. As we reached the table, he seemed on the verge of tears. His eyes flicked from one adult to the next.

"I hope he can give his talk," Mrs. Taylor said softly. She brought her hand to her face and flicked a tuft of hair back for about the hundredth time in the short time I had been around her.

"He'll do fine," Bart announced. "Won't you, Jimmy?"

I frowned at the way the adults were talking at him. With a slow motion, I sat my beer glass on the table. I folded my dress behind my legs and squatted down to be at his eye level. "My name is Mel. Short for Melissa." I held out my hand. "I hear you had a hard time at the hospital these past couple of months. Is that right?"

Jimmy slowly shook my hand and nodded. He glanced up at his parents then back to me.

"I had a little boy your age. He died. He was always scared around lots of grown ups too." I paused with a smile. "I hear you get to make us all listen to you. Is that right?"

"I have to give a talk," Jimmy said so softly it was barely whispered.

"Do you want to give this talk?"

"I guess." Jimmy glanced up at his parents. They were watching us interact. "I want to…"

I nodded waiting for him to finish.

"I want to thank the people who give money to help me and my friends at the hospital. Dr. Billy says that without their money, I'd be dead." Jimmy fiddled with his coat pocket then his collar. "What was your boy's name?"

"Robbie."

"Did he have leukemia too?"

"No. He died in a car accident."

Jimmy just looked at me with his big, round, brown eyes. "Did it hurt?"

"I don't know, he was asleep." I paused. "Does your treatment hurt?"

"Sometimes."

"I bet you're brave though, huh?"

Jimmy smiled. "Dr. Billy says I'm the bravest kid he's ever worked with." Jimmy's head came up with pride.

"You look brave and strong. I know it's tough doing what you have to do."

"The only part I don't like is not being able to play all the time," Jimmy said. He was no longer playing with his coat pocket. "I can't run as fast as the other kids, but I can beat them all in chess. Dad taught me to play chess when I was sick last year. Do you play?"

I nodded. "But not very well. I used to play in high school."

Jimmy smiled a huge smile. "I played a Chess Master a couple of weeks ago. I nearly beat him." He face lit up and he was talking in very animated tones. His words were coming fast and his voice was a lot louder than his previous whisper.

I nodded, listening to him tell me about his game. As he was moving his hands around, showing how the Chess Master had beat him, I felt someone watching me. I glanced up, but only his mom was still watching us. Bart and Mr. Taylor were speaking with another person. I returned my attention back to Jimmy. "Wow! I bet that was exciting."

"Oh it was. He said I played good for a six year old. Asked if maybe I might wanna see him play another Chess Master in the winter. Mom and Dad said that I could if I'm feeling good. Then Dr. Billy asked if I'd come here and talk tonight. At first I was really excited, but I don't know now." Jimmy's face fell as he looked around. He lowered his voice again. "I want to, but…"

"You're braver than me, Jimmy." I patted his shoulder. "I'd hate to get up there…" I pointed at the platform. "And talk in front of all these people. Talk about scary."

Jimmy shook his head. "I've done scarier things."

"Oh yeah? Like what?" I noticed that the crowd was beginning to sit down at the tables. And the platform was starting to fill also. Still, I had a feeling that someone was intently staring at us. I glanced around and saw Max standing near the end of the platform, next to an old lady, watching us. From the way the people were doting on her, she had to be Mrs. Grasicolli. My eyes lingered a second with Max, then I turned my attention back to Jimmy.

"Going to chemo and getting stuck with needles and everything, when I know that it will hurt, and when I know that I'm gonna be sick right after, and when I will not be able to play for days afterwards because I'll be sick, that's really scary, Mel."

I acted as though I thought about it. "You know, you're right. Talking to all of us stupid adults is not scary at all." I smiled. "Besides, you get to make us wait to eat, just to listen to you."

Jimmy laughed. "Yeah, no one ever listens to us. Now you have to listen to me."

"Not just me…" I paused and turning slightly, I motioned to the entire room. "All of us. You get to make all of us listen to you."

Jimmy laughed and clapped his hands. "I get to make you listen to me. I do." He leaned in close. "I like you. You're not like the other old people here."

I moved back half a step, still squatted down. "Old?!" I smirked. "Do I look old to you?"

Jimmy nodded. "Everyone here is old."

I chuckled. Glancing up, I saw that everyone was sitting down. I caught John's eye as he moved up next to me. And with a quick look, I noticed that Max was still watching us. "I think we need to sit down to eat, Jimmy." I stood up.

"Will you sit next to me?" Jimmy took my hand.

I glanced at his mother who nodded with a smile. "Sure, Jimmy. I'd like that a lot."

We sat down just as the MC was getting everyone's attention. He began to introduce people on the platform starting with Mrs. Grasicolli. Max got introduced, then down the line. He nodded at the crowd, but his eyes returned to my table.

Our eyes caught over the short distance; we were in the second row. His eyes softened just a bit as Jimmy lightly pounded on my arm. I let my eyes linger for just a second with Max then I turned my attention to the boy. He motioned for me to lean closer.

37

"I said I wasn't scared but I really am. All these people staring at me. Lots of people stare at me. People stare at me 'cause of my bald head. Do you think these people will laugh at me?" Jimmy whispered.

I shook my head. "Just think about making us wait to eat. I bet some of them are super hungry and they have to wait for you. You. I think that's funny."

Jimmy sort of smiled. "But I have to get up there." He pointed at the podium on the platform. "I…"

Max was once again watching us.

"See that man looking at us…" I pointed to Max.

Jimmy took a look then nodded.

"His name is Max. He's a friend of mine. Would you like to make him laugh, just him laugh, when you get up there? Would that be fun?"

Jimmy smiled.

I pulled Jimmy in closer and whispered in his ear. "Just say that the orchestra is missing its first chair. Can you remember that?"

Jimmy smiled from ear to ear. "Okay."

Everyone was looking at us now that Jimmy had been introduced. Jimmy gave his parents a shy look, then looked at me. I nodded with a smile. With a bit of reluctance, he walked up to the podium.

The MC had already placed a large stand so that Jimmy could reach the microphone and be seen over the table. He hesitated at the platform then looked at me. He first walked up to Mrs. Grasicolli and thanked her as he was supposed to do, according to his mom, who was softly coaching her son from her seat. She was more nervous than her boy.

Next Jimmy hesitated with a quick look at me again, then he moved up to Max. He motioned for Max to lean in close. With a bit of trepidation Max did, then his eyes flicked to me. His eyes widened slightly then crinkled up in delight. Max sat up with a slight red tint to his face and then he chuckled. As Jimmy moved to the podium, confident because Max had laughed, Max shook his finger at me.

I smiled back with a wink.

Bart leaned over. "What was that about?"

I gave him a dirty look but didn't respond. I saw John also looking at me from across the table with a puzzled look. I merely gave him a smile.

I turned my attention back to Jimmy who had started his speech. It was cute. He thanked everyone for donating money to help kids like himself, then he told of some of his friends still in the hospital, and their treatments and stories. At the end, Mrs. Grasicolli stood and gave Jimmy a hug.

The crowd gave him a nice round of applause. Right as Jimmy was moving off the platform, Max motioned him over. Now Max leaned over and whispered in Jimmy's ear. Jimmy nodded and walked back to the table as the meal was being served.

Max watched him, then looked at me. I gave him a puzzled look but waited until Jimmy was seated next to me. Jimmy looked up at Max who winked.

Jimmy pulled me into him. "He wants to know if you ever replaced the duckies."

I blushed now. Max is about the only person in the world who can get me to blush. I chuckled at Jimmy, then looked up at Max. He was not eating yet but watching our table.

Our eyes locked again. I shook my head as Bart was trying to get my attention by tapping my arm. I kept my eyes on Max, ignoring Bart. I could see that he still cared for me, it showed in his eyes. I mouthed to him, 'Can we talk?'

Max didn't answer. His expression stiffened although the fake smile remained on his face as he looked away. His grandmother said something to him, she looked puzzled. He replied to his grandmother, the fake smile still plastered on his face. Only then did I respond to Bart.

"What?"

Bart frowned then glanced up at the platform. "You need to speak with Mrs. Grasicolli."

"I know that Bart. I will. Right after the meal. Don't worry, you'll get your money's worth." I almost snarled at him in a whisper. I noticed John watching everything closely.

Jimmy was once more pounding on my arm.

"Yes?"

"You want to talk to the old lady?" He pointed to the platform.

I nodded. "Can you introduce me to Mrs. Grasicolli after the meal?"

"I can do that," Jimmy said with a huge grin on his face. "I'll hook you up."

I laughed. I was being helped in my work by a six year old cancer patient who was going to 'hook me up' with a potential source of information. Jimmy laughed with me. I lifted my eyes to the platform to find both Max and his grandmother staring at us. Max was intently watching me and Grasicolli was eyeing Jimmy with a smile.

***

"...and this is my new friend, Mel," Jimmy was telling Mrs. Grasicolli. In grandmotherly fashion, she gave him her full attention. She was shorter than me but carried her weight well. He had pulled me toward the platform after the meal. The band was playing soft jazz music in the background. The party itself would last until midnight, but we knew that she and her party would be leaving soon. I wanted to get the information and leave also. I was dead tired and starting to ache again.

"Mel?" Mrs. Grasicolli asked.

"Short for Melissa. I don't particularly like my full name."

Mrs. Grasicolli shook her fully gray head with a rueful grin. "It must be your age group. My grandson doesn't like his full name either."

"Well, Maximilian is quite a mouthful."

"Do you know my grandson?" She sipped at her mixed drink taking a glance around the area.

Jimmy was once more pounding on my arm. "Mel. Mel, I gotta go. Daddy is saying it's time." I glanced with him at Mr. Taylor who was motioning for the boy to come. "Dr. Billy doesn't want me to stay out too late. It makes me extra tired."

I once more folded up my dress and squatted down to be at his level. "Thank you for you help, Jimmy."

"You're welcome. Will you come and visit me sometime?"

"I sure will. I'll call your mom and dad and we'll arrange a time to get together."

Jimmy stepped half a step back and gave me a condescending look. "You're just kidding. You won't come and see me."

I put my elbow on my knee and rested my chin on my fist. "Now why do you say that?"

"I just know. You don't even know where I live."

"I'm a private detective. I bet I can find out where you live."

"You are not!"

"I am. Tell you what… I'll find out where you live and send you a surprise. How about that?"

"Really?"

A voice drifted into our conversation. "If Mel says she will Jimmy, you can bet she will."

We both looked up to see Max standing next to his grandmother smiling. Mrs. Grasicolli was watching and smiling too.

"Okay." Jimmy quickly looked at his Dad. "I'll be waiting. You sure? You promise? Cross your heart, hope to die promise?"

I crossed my heart. "I promise."

"Okay." Jimmy turned to go, then swiftly turned back and threw his arms around me. His little arms clung tightly around my neck for a second.

I closed my eyes and swallowed hard. I still missed Robbie with all my heart. I cleared my throat. "I promise Jimmy."

Jimmy stepped away. "You'd make a great Mom. I bet Robbie was really happy that you were his mom." With that, he ran away waving.

I stayed squatted down for a brief second, composing myself. Jimmy had touched a part of me that I thought had healed, at least a little. But it hadn't. The pain was deep and searing still. I was told that the pain of losing a child never goes away. I hoped one day it got easier. As I stood, I took a breath.

"That was sweet, Melissa. Oh, I'm sorry, Mel," Mrs. Grasicolli corrected herself.

I pulled my eyes away from Jimmy to find Max staring me in the eyes. I could see that the hard edge was gone. There was maybe even understanding in them.

"Jimmy said you wanted to talk to me. He said he needed to 'hook us up.'" Her smile was a genuine one. She was not the pretentious snob that I thought she might be.

I chuckled. "Kids say the funniest things."

"I take it you have children."

"I did." I glanced at Max. "My son was killed in a car accident when he was five."

Mrs. Grasicolli patted my arm. "It's hard losing a child, be it to disease or an accident."

"How are you doing with that?" Max asked. His hands were now stuck firmly in his pockets. His sky blue eyes were holding mine. He looked genuinely interested.

I shrugged. "Some days are better than others. Most days are pretty good. Then something will spark the pain..." I nodded in the direction that Jimmy had gone in.

"I saw you with him. He really opened up to you."

"He was scared of all these people. I think the tuxes and formal dresses and stuff spooked him. Not to mention being the only kid here." I paused. "I just reached out and let him know that we adults aren't any different than him. That the same thing scares us too."

Max's eyes lightened even more. He motioned with his arm to a roving waiter and procured two wine glasses. He offered one to me.

I took it with a thank you nod.

"So, how do the two of you know each other?" Mrs. Grasicolli asked us. She was mostly speaking to Max though.

Max didn't answer for a long couple of seconds. His eyes just staring into mine. "Grandma, this is Mel from Illinois. The one I told you about."

Mrs. Grasicolli's head snapped back to look at me. Her eyes slightly hardened. "So, you're the one who broke my Maximilian's heart."

My eyes flicked to Max who blushed a tint of red. I held up my hand to Max, who opened his mouth to speak. "I didn't mean to, Mrs. Grasicolli. I really didn't. I tried to call him and apologize, but he refused to answer my calls. I even tracked him to Texas but... Anyway, yes, I did. And I'm sorry. It had been just at a year from the car accident that claimed my husband and my son. I wasn't ready for..." I shrugged at her as she began nodding her head. Now I only looked at Max. "I'm sorry for running out on you that way. I got spooked." Our eyes stayed locked for a brief second, then he studied his shoes.

The tension increased as I panned my eyes past Mrs. Grasicolli then out into the crowd. My attention was caught by John standing near the door. He tapped his watch. I nodded at him.

Turning back to the two of them, I saw Max still contemplating his footwear and Mrs. Grasicolli staring at him. "Look Mrs. Grasicolli, I only wanted to ask you a question, if I could. Then I'll be out of both of your hair." My eyes flicked to Max who was still not looking up.

The elderly lady turned to me. Her tone was colder than before, but she seemed to understand where I was coming from. "Yes?"

"I work for a Private Investigator firm in Quincy Illinois. We're looking for a lady who was supposedly in your employ here at Griffin Industries a long time ago. About fifteen years ago. She disappeared and, well, someone needs to find her. I was wondering if you might have any idea where she might be?"

"Who?"

"Ava Papios," I said watching her for any reaction. All I saw was puzzlement. I really hadn't expected anything else. Griffin Industries was a big company even back then. And probably she wasn't involved in the day to day running of the business, let alone getting to know a secretary. Especially back when there were not as many women in the work place. Most likely it would have been Mr. Grasicolli that would have remembered Ava, but we knew he was deceased. Or maybe one of the assorted executive managers would have remembered, but even that was a long shot.

"Ava Papios?" Mrs. Grasicolli repeated softly. She seemed to be running the name through her head, then she shook it. "No. I did help with this business, that's why it still has a special place in my heart, but no I don't recall any such name. Can you describe her? And why is this person looking for her? And just so you know, I only vaguely knew anyone here beyond management."

"I figured as much. However, we needed to start somewhere. She worked in human resources, maybe a secretary for managers." With a quick movement, I produced an old picture of the lady in question.

43

"This is her about thirty years ago. I know it's not much to go on." I handed it to her, then a second one. "This is a computer simulation of what she might have looked like twenty years ago and possibly now."

Max looked at the pictures then at me. "Who is the client?"

I hesitated just a fraction of a second. Normally I wouldn't release our client's name, but I wanted Max to know that I wasn't here on a date. "Bart Hessor. He's been trying to find her for a long number of years. He recently discovered that there is a… discrepancy in his family history and she possibly played a role in it. Hessor is trying to find her to confirm who his actual parents are." Max was once more studying the picture. I turned my attention back to the older lady. "My associates and I have tracked her to your business, then the trail dead ends. I was hoping you could help us."

"I don't recognize her," Mrs. Grasicolli said, still looking at the two pictures. "But as I said, I didn't do much with the business. I sat on the board, still do in name. My late husband did more during the merger."

I watched as Max studied the pictures then glanced at his grandmother. "I understand. Is it possible that we might get permission to see her old personnel file to possibly find a clue as to where she might have disappeared to?"

"Well, I—"

"So, you aren't here on a date then?" He looked at me, his blue eyes now a liquid blue.

I shook my head. "You should know better, Max. Bart was my meal ticket here. You saw John at our table. He's here to make sure Bart stays in line." I paused nodding with my head in John's direction. "John found out that several of her old, fellow employees that she used to hang out with were here tonight. We hoped she might show up. One man mentioned that a bunch of them were getting together."

Max's eyes flicked to the door, and he gave a head bob to John.

"I'm sorry I can't help you, Mel." Mrs. Grasicolli handed the pictures back. "But I will call the executive manager here, Bob Tanger, and tell him to let you have access to her file."

I accepted the pictures. "Thanks. It's still a long shot, but it's the only lead we have."

Max grabbed my hand with the pictures. "Can I take them with me?"

I let go quickly. His finger tips on mine were almost burning my hand. I felt heat in other parts of my body as well. "Sure. Why?"

"Dad worked for a while cleaning up some problems here at Griffin, if I recall." He turned to his grandmother. "Wasn't this the only business in St. Louis at the time?"

Mrs. Grasicolli nodded. "I believe so."

"Then it would have been around the time I remember Dad staying in St. Louis. I spent a couple of weeks with him. I'll ask him the next time I talk to him."

"Thanks."

Max's eyes softened. "Not a problem."

Mrs. Grasicolli glanced at her grandson then at me. Our eyes were still locked, but I saw her out of the corner of my eye. "Nice to meet you, Mel. I need to go speak to someone." She quickly disappeared from our side.

"I'm sorry, Max. I was pretty shaken up by everything that happened."

Max didn't respond. Even his eyes seemed to be back to neutral.

"It's no excuse but…" I shrugged. "You moved too fast. I wasn't ready."

"I see."

I sat the glass of wine on the table. I hadn't even sipped out of it. When I turned back, he was still studying me.

"And now?"

"Honestly?"

He nodded. His expression had not changed. I had no idea what he was thinking.

"I don't know." I looked away to stare at the floor. "You were right about Craig. And about me forgiving him but not myself." I looked up to see his blue eyes piercing me. "I have since gone to see someone about… things. Mostly about my anger." I gave him a slight grin.

Max's eyes widened. "You actually listened?"

"Shut up." I grinned even bigger.

Max sort of smiled. "I'm glad."

"Yeah. I don't know if it did any good, but I went." I looked down at my feet again. "I miss you, Max. I miss the phone calls." I brought my eyes up to meet his and thought that I glimpsed a bit of the old Max. "I'd still like to be friends, if nothing else."

"Maybe."

"Getting closer to a yes?"

Max's face lit up in amusement. "Closer."

"So, you've forgiven me?"

"Not yet."

"Okay. I can handle that. I messed up. I still want to be your friend…" I watched as Max's attention was drawn behind me. His expression instantly hardened. I swiveled around to see Bart Hessor standing there.

Bart moved in next to me and put his arm around my waist. "Did you find out anything, Mel?"

I politely took his arm off my waist. "What did John tell you?"

Bart laughed. "Huddleston doesn't scare me. Besides, it' just an arm. It's not like I kissed you or anything. Unless you want to?" He smirked at Bauer.

Max's face remained stone hard with that fake smile plastered on. And the eyes were narrow and ice cold, glacier cold. He was staring at Hessor. "Still selling drugs?"

Bart turned his attention to Max. His eyes became hard and beady. "None of your business."

"Maybe I'll make it my business."

Bart bristled then gave Max a smile. "Try." He looked down at me. "Ready to head back to town?" His hand once more tucked around my waist.

I grabbed his wrist and quickly took his hand off my waist again. I held it in a grip from Judo to control people. I looked Bart in the eyes. "Not again Bart or this will get ugly here and now. And I'll be vocal about where your money comes from." I gave one last squeeze at which Bart flinched, then I released him. I turned back to Max. "Thanks for your help. Call sometime if you want. My number hasn't changed." With a smile at Max, I walked away.

46

I deliberately didn't look back as I walked. I instead was watching John, who was staring at the guys. His eyes flicked to me and then behind me again. Something was going on, but I was not going to turn around. But, curiosity got the better of me. I swiveled my head to peek. Then I came to a full stop and watched.

Max was in Bart's face. The smile was still plastered in place, but even at this distance I could see his eyes were stone cold. He was talking slowly. I had seen him do this one other time when he was pissed.

Finally Bart spoke back to Max then turned and walked toward me. I saw Max give John some sort of guy communication look, then he turned and moved to his grandmother's side. I looked at Hessor; he was not happy. His smile was fake too, but the eyes were beady hard. And they were staring directly at me.

I met John at the door, and we quickly walked toward the exit. Neither of us spoke. Bart caught up with us before we hit the doors.

"What did Grasicolli say?" Bart asked me as we exited the building, anger still in his voice.

"I'll give you a full report tomorrow," John said as his hand landed in the small of my back and gave a little nudge to keep me going while he stopped and faced Bart.

"I just want to know—"

"Tomorrow. I'll call you and we'll meet." John said and started walking toward me.

I looked back to see that Bart had stopped just outside the door. John reached my side near the valet parking attendant and handed him the ticket. John nudged me again, and I turned back around. We stood there in silence waiting until the car came to a stop in front of us.

"He's still watching," I whispered to John.

John said nothing but opened my door then rounded the car. John pulled away from the center, and I looked back to see Bart head inside. We turned the corner before John spoke. "What was that about?"

"What was what?" I asked as I took off my pumps.

"Between Max and Hessor?"

"I don't know." I glanced down at my hands. I was pretty sure I could guess what had been said, but I preferred not to think about it.

John grunted in disapproval but didn't comment further on the subject. "Between the two of us, we spoke with all of the older folks there. Get any leads?"

"One person remembered her. She was a secretary and worked for a manager that left shortly after she did. Didn't remember the manager's name though." I slipped my tennis shoes on, and as I tied them I continued. "Mrs. Grasicolli gave us permission to search Papios' personnel file. I'll call Bob Tanger in a couple of days. You?"

"Similar story. I got the name of an executive that might remember the name of the manager she worked for but nothing else."

"So it wasn't a total waste of time. Maybe there'll be something in her files that'll tell us where she went next." Not to mention that I might have opened the door to mending fences with Max. If for no other reason, it was a success.

"Maybe." John concentrated on driving in the St. Louis traffic.

I closed my eyes, and soon the hum of his car and the vibration of the drive knocked me out.

Chapter 6

On Saturday, I was just returning from a skiing trip on the Mississippi with Mitch and his friends, when I got a call on my cell to come to the Silver Moon, my dad's bar. Someone wanted to talk to me. I hoped it was Ralph about the farm property. I was getting nervous that we weren't coming up with clues. It felt like each day that passed, the chances of finding Carmen decreased.

I hopped out of the jeep and threw a t-shirt on over my bathing suit. It was hot and muggy again. July in Illinois was like living in a Turkish bath house. My cut off jeans were still wet from the water, but it felt really good. I glanced up at the recently vacant apartment above the bar that I used to live in. Sometimes I missed living there, but I didn't today. The air conditioner at my new house worked so much better than the window unit in my old apartment.

My eyes hadn't adjusted to the dim interior of the bar, and as I walked in, the cool air blasted me, so I waited for a couple of seconds before moving farther in. I could hear Dad at the far end talking with someone. I rubbed my eyes and looked around. There wasn't anyone that I recognized, and Ralph wasn't there. Dad stood up from a lean and walked back toward me behind the bar.

"Hi Sweetie."

"Hi Dad. Where's this person who wants to see me?" I looked around.

Dad winked with a gleam in his eye. "He went to the bathroom. Want a beer?"

I shook my head. I was driving, and I needed to head home as soon as I was done here. I scooted onto the nearest barstool. "I'll take a water though."

"Coming up." He headed to the appropriate cooler case.

A body slid up next to me at the bar. "Hi, Mel."

I turned quickly. "Max!" I knew the smile that hit my face was huge, so I quickly tried to tone it down. "What are you doing here?" I involuntarily looked him over.

He was in dress slacks, a type of chino, with a light blue polo shirt that made his blue eyes glow in the muted light of the bar. His shoes were brown loafers of some sort. As always he was dressed impeccably.

Max chuckled. He laid the two pictures on the bar in front of me. He motioned to my dad in the universal 'one more' sign and dad nodded. "Returning your pictures."

My smile faded a bit more. "Okay. Did you find out anything from your dad?"

A negative shake was the answer. "He doesn't remember her, but after looking at his files, he gave me the name of an old manager that used to work there. According to Dad, this guy knew everyone and everything that happened." Max reached into his pocket and pulled out a piece of paper. He put it on top of the photos, then finished off his soda. His eyes were watching and calculating, I could tell.

Dad set my bottle of water and Max's soda on the bar, then hurried to help another customer. I glanced at the paper. A name and phone number. It was a start. Taking a drink of my own bottle, I nodded. "Thanks."

"Not a problem."

I opened my mouth to speak but my cell rang. I quickly checked the display. Ralph Zimmerman. "I gotta take this, Max… Ralph, buddy. What did you find out?"

Max watched me as he got more comfortable on the stool. He looked around the bar then back at me.

I smiled as I listened.

"No one has seen either of them. That farm is a pretty big place. I talked with Mrs. Crabtree. She hasn't actually been on the property for years."

50

"Will she give us permission to look the property over? We just want to see if… well, I don't know really. I guess just to look the area over." What we wanted to do was look to see if there were any fresh diggings. We had discussed just trespassing on the property, figuring no one would know, but decided to wait to see if we could get legal permission.

"She seemed undecided."

"Will she talk to me?"

"I doubt it. She's got agoraphobia, a fear of leaving her house. She hasn't left the house in ages and really doesn't like to talk to too many people either. And won't let very many people in her house, especially strangers. Myself, her nurse, and the Meals on Wheels people are the only ones she talks to as far as I know. Won't even really talk to her doctor." Ralph chuckled. "Don't know why she picked me. Guess it's 'cause I cut their grass since I was in grade school. Always have cut her grass. Go figure. She doesn't like to use the phone either. I'm headed over there now. She's got a leaky pipe or something. I'll try to convince her. I'll call you back."

"Thanks, Ralph. I owe you one on this."

"I'll take you up on it. We need a babysitter real soon. I'll call and let you know when you get to watch my three kids."

"I'm only giving you one night of my time, unless you make it worth my while."

"You drive a hard bargain. I'll get back to you." The phone disconnected.

Max was still just looking at me. His eyes guarded, almost wary.

"I'm exchanging babysitting for some information." I slugged down another big drink of cold water while Max's expression changed to an almost smile.

Dad was now standing behind the bar near us. "Did you ever find anything with that missing kid, Mel?"

"Not yet. I'm trying to get permission to enter the property."

Dad shook his head as he walked away. "Sick people."

Max squirreled up his face in puzzlement.

"We got a call from a PI in New Jersey. He thinks that a father snitched his eight year old girl from her mom and is hiding out some where here in Illinois. We've narrowed it down to a seven hundred acre farm. It doesn't look too promising. Rich thinks the girl is already dead."

"Killed by the dad?"

I nodded solemnly. "Yeah, but we can't find him either."

Max merely shook his head.

"How long are you in town for?" My heart was beating faster again as I waited for his answer.

Max shrugged.

I glanced at my watch. It was after five in the evening. "Can I buy you supper? Or have you already eaten?"

The blue eyes stared into mine. The edge was back. I had no idea what he was thinking or feeling.

"Or not." I shrugged. "I thought I'd pick up some Maid Rites and head home, or we could eat at the restaurant if you would feel more comfortable there."

He grimaced. "Thanks for reminding me of the hamburgers. Now I have a craving for one."

I smiled. "I knew you didn't come here to see me."

Max tried to hide his smile with his soda can. "I understand that you don't live above the bar anymore."

"Yep. I moved out. Dad is trying to rent the place to someone else."

"Where do you live?"

"About three miles from here. I bought a small complex with one of the settlements from the accident, and now I rent out the apartments." I paused. "I had an aunt that once told me that if I found a good apartment complex to own, I'd never have to work another day in my life. She lied. The apartments take up more of my time than working for Rich and John."

Max chuckled again. "You a landlady?"

"Yeah. It's already paying for itself." I sat the bottle on the bar. "Well Max, supper? I owe you that much for getting me this guy's name." I picked up the photos.

"Yeah, you do."

"Good. I've got an errand to run. Do you want to meet at the restaurant or eat at my place or what?"

Max considered. "I'll pick up the food and meet you at your place. Where is it?"

I gave him the address and reached into my pocket for a twenty. "Here. Get my usual. Do you remember what it is?" At Max's nod, I continued. "Give me half an hour to do this errand, and I'll meet you at my house." I stood up and patted his back gently. "Thanks."

As I walked out, I rubbed my hand on my jeans. It was tingling.

***

I was standing in the parking lot of the apartment four-plex talking with Mitch. He and Kick had brought the boat from the river this afternoon and they were parking it in my back lot. Kick already left, but Mitch and I were still talking.

"If she lets you on the property, what are you going to do?" Mitch asked as he leaned on his car next to me.

I looked down at the asphalt and crossed my arms. "Rich thinks the girl is dead and the dad is hiding out on the property."

"Why?"

"He heard of a man seen coming and going. So far we can't even get a glimpse of the man." I could feel Mitch's stare. I looked up. "What?"

"This is not going to sit well with you. Especially if you find a body."

I stood up off the car and looked down at my shoes again. "I know. But now I feel obligated. Rich didn't even want me to know about it."

Mitch nodded.

I stuck my hands in the pockets of my cutoffs and kicked a pebble out of the way. My feelings had been going in circles with this case. I should never have taken that call from Wanda Carson.

Mitch's head snapped up to look at my driveway across the parking lot. His eyes narrowed. "Who drives a silver Beemer?"

I looked at him then followed his gaze across the lot. A brand new silver BMW was pulling into the lot. It's windows were tinted, not letting us see who was driving. "I dunno. Doesn't belong to any of my tenants."

It stopped not far from us. The door opened and Max stepped out.

Mitch grinned, and it got even bigger when he looked at me. We both took a couple of steps to reach the car.

"Shoot, Bauer. Quit the force in California and hit the big time. What did you do, win the lottery?"

Max smiled at Mitch, and they shook hands. "Something like that. How are you doing, Mitch?"

Mitch was now admiring the car. "Not bad, not bad, but not as good as you. Nice." His eyes still running up and down the classy car.

"It's not mine actually. It's leased to my company."

My brother's head snapped up. "Your company?"

Max glanced at me then turned his attention back to Mitch. "Yeah. I inherited it from my grandfather when he passed away three months ago. They make liners for oil tankers, and other things including international shipping."

Mitch laughed. "Must make a lot of money."

"A ton," Max said, then reached in and grabbed the brown paper bags from the front floor board. "Supper."

Mitch shook his head. He had that brotherly look in his eyes as he glanced at Max. He glanced at his watch. "I gotta go. Tina is waiting on me. Good to see you again, Max. Take it slow, WT."

I caught his eye and let him know that I was okay. "Drive safely, boogger head." I heard Mitch's laugh all the way off the lot.

Max watched Mitch leave then turned back to me. "Take it slow?" His eyes betrayed his concern.

I looked at Max before answering. "Yeah." I let it drop. It was obvious that Max wanted nothing more than friendship. He probably had another woman in his life. I couldn't imagine him being long without someone, especially after learning about his grandmother and family. Rich men didn't stay alone for long. I motioned for Max to follow. We walked away from the two story building toward a smaller house next door.

Max gave a glance at the apartment complex then followed carrying the bags. "I thought you said—"

"I said…" I turned as I walked. "That I bought a complex. I didn't say I lived in it." I smiled. "The house came with the complex. More private." I held open the gate for him, then followed him into the yard.

The back yard was grassy and shaded with three big oak trees. My house was a standard brick ranch style house. The deck extended off the back right above the ground. On one end of the deck sat a gazebo with hot tub, that was also attached to the deck. Sitting on the deck was a table and chair set with umbrella and a grill to the side. I motioned for Max to set the bags on the table.

"Since we're actually getting a breeze, I thought we might eat outside. If that's okay with you?"

"Sure."

"What do you want to drink?"

"Soda."

"Have a seat. I'll be right back." I headed inside. When I returned with drinks, he had the Maid Rites out of the bags and the cheddar crisps and French fries split between us. I sat down across from to him with a smile.

"Thanks," Max said taking the soda.

"No. Thanks for picking up the sandwiches." I had just dug into one when my phone rang. "Yeah?" I moved the food to the side of my mouth as I answered the phone.

"Mrs. Crabtree said it was okay for you to search the property. Just don't damage any of it. There's an easy access road off of Bangers Point road if you don't want to park at the rental house."

I swallowed quickly. "Thanks, Ralph. I appreciate the help."

"We're thinking next Saturday night. From like four o'clock to midnight or so. I'd like to take Martha out for supper and a movie or something."

"Let me check my schedule, but I think it's okay." I hung up and immediately dialed Rich's number. I glanced at Max. "I'll be done in a minute…" I got Rich's answering service and left a message about what Ralph had told me.

The rest of the meal was eaten in mostly silence. It was sort of tense. I wondered why he was here and what he wanted from me.

Max finished first and leaned back in his chair to study me.

I finished with my sandwich and munched on my half of the cheddar crisps watching him watch me. "What?"

"I was just wondering how you really are?"

I stared into Max's eyes. "About the whole thing with Craig, okay. About Robbie's death, not so fine. I still have my days. The doctor says that's normal. This missing kid case has thrown me for a loop. Then Jimmy in St. Louis."

Max nodded in understanding. "Did you send him anything yet?"

"Yeah. I bought the biggest Lego set I could find online. Had it shipped overnight." I noticed Max smiled. "Robbie was just getting into building with Legos. I figured Jimmy was probably into them too. I got a call from him yesterday. He was really happy." I looked out over the backyard, my heart hurting and my gut twisting. Suddenly I needed to move, to do something. I stood up quickly and gathered the trash.

"Mel…"

I looked at him.

"It's okay to cry." His blue eyes were soft and light. His face no longer had the hard edge to it.

"I know. Jimmy's dad told me that the night they got home from the fundraiser there was a message on their machine. Jimmy is no longer in remission." I held his eyes for a brief second then walked inside to throw away the trash. I returned with a beer for myself. "Want a beer?"

"No."

I sat. "I like the beard and moustache."

Max fingered it, running his hands over his chin.

"It makes you look…" I couldn't think of any term but 'sexy' and I didn't want to say that.

"Sexy?"

I blushed. "Yeah."

"I know. I hear it all the time." Max gave me a wry grin.

"Is there someone in your life now?" I took another drink of beer to cover the worried look. I might as well find out, as much as it would hurt. Better to get it out in the open.

Max merely studied me and didn't answer. He let the silence drag out. Our eyes were locked in a sort of war. He was very hard to read. I could tell that he was still hurting from the way I had left him. Max opened his mouth but was interrupted by a voice from beyond the wood gate.

"Mel?"

I almost sighed. "Come on in, Rich."

The gate was already swinging open. Rich smiled at us sitting there. He nodded in acknowledgment at Max. "John told me you were in St. Louis. How are you doing, Max?"

"Fine."

Rich sat down. "I got your message. I also arranged to have Kevin and his dogs from Springfield come in tonight. They're on their way and should be here in less than an hour. We still have a good three hours of daylight. I was going to see if you wanted to do some exploring but…" He glanced at Max then back to me with a knowing look.

"Well…?"

"Dogs?" Max asked finishing off his soda.

Rich nodded. "Has Mel told you about the missing kid case?" At Max's nod he continued, "I've got a feeling the kid is dead. Carmen's been missing for six months and rumor has it her dad, Brady Carson, has been here for two. Kevin is with the State Police and has access to cadaver dogs. He's going to work as much of the property as we can tonight that's away from the rental house. I hope we don't find anything but…"

"How many people do you have to look?" Max asked.

"Well, John and me. Mitch, Larry and Kick all just volunteered. Mitch is going to see if the explorer scouts will head that way. If so, about fifteen to twenty total, not counting Mel."

Max looked at me. He inclined his head to Rich.

"I would if you weren't here, but I don't think—"

Max interrupted me. "Count me in, I guess. I'll need to change out of these dress slacks."

Rich smiled. "Good. Meet us at Banger's Point Road in forty minutes. Bring your Jeep, we might need it in a couple of spots." Rich stood up to leave. "You know Mel, we've got a pot going that you actually find the body."

"Bite me, Rich."

Rich laughed all the way to the gate. "See ya," was thrown over his shoulder at us.

Max was smiling, almost laughing.

"You know, you don't have to do this."

"I know." He stood up. "Are you going let me use your bathroom to change?"

"Sure."

I headed into the house while Max went through the back gate to get a small piece of luggage from the car. It wasn't long and we were both changed and ready to go. I had assembled on the kitchen table several items for the night: two backpacks, two flashlights, water containers in each, several snack items and lastly rubber gloves.

Max entered the kitchen and picked up the gloves. "Do you really think you're going to find the girl?"

"I think she's alive. I'm doing this to rule out that she's buried on the farm," I said still working on a backpack. "Can you think of anything else we might need?"

"A GPS unit would be good, so we don't get lost," Max said hefting one of the packs. He had on jeans and a white T-shirt. What looked like brand new white tennis shoes were on his feet.

I shook my head. "I don't have one."

"You can borrow mine." He looked me up and down.

I was dressed in jeans and a tank top with a short sleeved denim shirt over it. My hiking boots were laced up and ready to go. I snapped my fingers. "Bug spray."

"Excellent thought. If I recall, the bugs will be swarming this time of the year," Max said as I moved to the kitchen cabinet under the sink. "You've got a nice place."

I looked up from my squat by the sink. "Thanks." Something tickled my hand and as I looked back, I noticed a spider crawling across my fingers. I shrieked and landed on my butt. I shook my hand, scooting on my butt farther away from the sink with another shriek.

Max moved quickly, stomping on the spider. Then he looked at me and started laughing, a hold-your-belly, tears-in-the-eyes kind of laugh. He ended up leaning on the counter he was laughing so hard.

I took several deep breaths while he laughed, trying to calm my nerves. "It's not funny. I hate spiders. That scared the begeebers out of me." I took another deep breath to calm myself and rubbed the back of my hand where the spider had crawled.

Max was still laughing, although he was trying to get himself under control. His laugh lines made him even more handsome.

I pulled my eyes away from his handsomeness to look back under my sink. "I'm going to need to get an exterminator. That was a huge spider."

"For one itty bitty spider?" Max managed to get out between guffaws.

I finally stood up. I gave him a dirty look. "Stop laughing, Bauer."

"You shrieked," Max said, wiping his eyes. "I've never heard you shriek like a girl before."

"I hate spiders." I grabbed one of the packs off the table and headed out the door.

Max followed, grabbing the other, still smiling. I locked up and we headed to the parking lot. After retrieving the GPS unit from his car, I handed Max the keys to the Jeep.

He held them in his open hand and looked puzzled.

"I've had two beers. I could drive, but I think it's better this way. Do you mind?"

He hesitated a second. "No, but you'll have to give me directions." He hopped into the Jeep. "By the way, nice paint job." The sarcasm was evident in his voice along with the smile in his eyes.

My car had recently been hit. I was waiting on insurance to get it painted. I coughed softly and cleared my throat. "Thanks. I like the beat up look. Makes it less vulnerable to theft."

Max chuckled and started it up. I hopped in after, making sure the packs were secure. We buckled up and he pulled into the street.

***

Max, myself and two explorer scouts were searching a distant part of the wooded farm area. Since there wasn't even a well defined road, merely an old two track, to get to the field on the far side of the farm, we used the Jeep. This time I drove. Now we fanned out, and although keeping each other in sight, we were walking in a line across a small field.

I wiped the sweat off my face and took off my short sleeved shirt. I bundled it up and stuck it in the pack. Then I started again. The mosquitoes were out in full force and the bug spray only deterred them for a while. I saw Max swat at a couple. We had been at this three hours already. We were calling it a night as the sun was setting, but the kids, Max and I had agreed to finish this field.

The field itself hadn't been ploughed in several years. There were small trees growing in it, as nature tried to reclaim the ground with quick growing shrubs and trees. The weeds were tall, and I was sure we'd have ticks up the ying-yang when we got back. Finally, we made it to the end and gathering around one corner, caught our breath.

I handed candy bars to the teens who were sitting on the ground resting. Max was sitting too. He wiped the sweat off his forehead. I looked around.

My eyes passed over a small clump of woods at the apex of two blocks of woods, then drifted back. *Is that some sort of wood structure in the middle?* I looked at it in the waning sunlight, but it was really hard to tell. "Stay here a minute," I said and noticed the teens nodded like that was fine with them. I took off at a jog to check it out before we lost all light.

By the time I reached the small area, I heard someone following me. A quick glance showed it was Max.

"Slow up," he said with a tone. "Did you see something?"

"Nah, just I…" I looked at him as he caught up. "This caught my eye." I pointed at the area we were near. The trees were very close together here at the point of woods. "I thought it was a structure, but it was just a bunch of trees."

Max wiped his face. "Man, I haven't done this kind of hiking in a long time."

"Me too." I smiled at Max as he was currently looking at my chest. "Come on, Bauer. Let's check this out, then get the teens back to civilization."

Max smiled and motioned for me to take lead.

60

I stepped into the woods and picked my way through some bushes. I took another step and started falling. The ground beneath my feet just fell away. I clawed at weeds and trees that kept breaking in my hands. Finally after what seemed an eternity, I felt a hand grab my shirt. It started ripping. Then another hand found my hand and the grip tightened on my wrist.

"Hold still," Max said in a low tone. He was struggling with something himself. "Stay still."

I did, I think, and tried focusing on his face. He was scrambling to gain a better foothold. Finally he must have been secure. I was still dangling, feet into nothingness. My heart was pounding faster than it had ever done. It felt like it was coming out of my chest. I had both hands gripping his one hand. My fingers were white I was holding on so hard.

"Mel, look at me… Mel?"

I heard him at a distance, as though in a tunnel. The sound of my own breathing and heart were so much louder. I was staring up at him.

"Mel!"

I blinked. The white disappeared to be replaced with Max's face.

"Stop kicking your feet. Calm down!" Max now had both of his hands on mine. "Look at me!"

I did.

"Use your feet and push up."

Let go? Why would I let go? I shook my head. No way. I was not letting go for nothing. I tightened my grip.

"Your feet! What is wrong with you? Use your…" Max's face was a scowl until suddenly a light seemed to go off in his head. He blinked. "Mel…" His tone changed as did his face. He was now almost smiling. "Look at me. Trust me. You won't fall. Even if you did, it's not that far, Tiger. Use your feet and push up."

I glanced past Max to the trees then focused on his face again. "Feet?" I managed to squeeze out of my tight throat.

"Tiger, look me in the eye. I won't let go. You're safe. I have you. Trust me. Move your feet. That's it," Max coached me. He pulled up on my arms.

I slowly began to regain control of my thoughts. I pushed up with my feet on the side of the hole or whatever. My eyes were locked with his, it was the only way I could do this. My heart beat was still loud in my ears.

"That's it. Just a little bit more… There we go, Tiger," Max said as he pulled me over the edge and farther from the area.

I felt him moving me to the ground, and I bent over a small tree. He was still smiling at me.

"You can let go of my hand now." He shook my hand to get me to loosen it. "Deep breaths."

I did. And with oxygen, my thoughts seemed to come. I coughed twice. I let go of Max and laid all the way back on the ground. It was at this time I realized that the two Explorer scouts were standing next to us. All I could do was take deep breaths and watch their concerned faces.

"Slow your breathing," Max said squatting down next to me. "That's it, Tiger." He looked up at the concerned teens. "We found a hole."

They both blew out their breath. One spoke looking at me, "We thought something bad happened with the blood curdling yell we heard."

"It just caught Mel by surprise," Max said with a wink at me.

I cursed softly. It wasn't really audible, but he knew what I had said or at least the intent.

Max laughed. "Just lay here for a minute, Mel."

I sat up. I looked around to see everyone still watching me. "I'm fine." I stood up.

"Mel, you're white as a sheet," Max said as he stood with me.

"I'm fine!"

Max held out his hands in surrender. "Fine. You're fine."

I moved closer to the hole again. I inched my way closer. Then I peered over the edge, my heart once more in my throat. It wasn't a long drop. Just about ten feet, give or take. I looked down again with a big swallow. No vertigo like I expected, just a little tightening in my stomach.

"Anything?" Max asked as he moved closer too.

I gave him a dirty look for getting that close to me and the hole, then I shook my head. "I don't know. I think there's something down there…" I turned him around, unzipped the pack that he was still wearing and felt around until I pulled out the flashlight.

I aimed it at the deepest area. Something flashed white, like a sycamore branch. I brought the light beam back to it. Max moved closer to the lip of the hole.

"Only you." He turned to face me, a serious look on his face.

"Ah, man."

I had found another body.

Chapter 7

Max and I sat in the darkening field waiting. The two explorer scouts ran back to where the Jeep was to show Rich and Kevin where we were. Kevin had called in the State Police.

I was looking at my shoes thinking when Max interrupted me.

"It's not the girl."

"I know. Those are just bones. It could be an old grave site. People used to get buried on their farms all the time."

"Then what are you thinking so intently?"

"Just working though some information in my mind. I think I'm going to go talk to the lady that rents the farm again. I think she's lying to me about something. I just wish I could pinpoint what it is."

Max didn't answer but laid down in the grassy area we were sitting in. He put his hands under his head, crossed his ankles and glanced at me after looking at the stars. "So, you're afraid of heights."

I blushed.

Max smiled.

"So?"

"And you're afraid of spiders."

"So?"

"It's not something I would have associated with you."

"What do you mean?"

"Since the first time I met you, you come off as a woman that knows what she likes, goes after it without a second thought, and damn the consequences." Max paused still looking at me, then turned his attention back to the sky. "I would never have thought you to be scared of anything."

The silence drug out for a while.

"I'm scared of a lot of things." I looked down at the ground.

"Yeah?"

"Yeah." I fiddled with the zipper on the backpack. Pulling out the denim shirt, I put it on, then I heard people talking. It must be Rich and company. I looked at Max before standing up. "I just know how to hide it well."

Max watched me stand, then finally stood himself.

Sure enough, Rich and a whole group of people were heading our way. Rich and John were already smiling.

"Our body finder," John said as they got within earshot.

I flipped him off. "It's not the girl though."

The two detectives exchanged a look.

Max nodded in agreement with me. "It's just bones. The flesh wouldn't decay that fast even here in this humid climate."

Rich cursed softly. "Not that I want her dead."

I showed the group where the bones were. We stood around discussing the situation. The guys agreed it could be an old grave site. Kevin got on his cell and asked the other cops to come as quietly as possible so as not to spook the guy from the woods, if he was even there.

By the time we left the scene, it was close to midnight. I was aching from the day on the river and now all this hiking. As we pulled into my lot, I was debating what to do. Max hopped out and stood near the Jeep. I handed him the GPS unit.

He took it and held my eyes.

"Do you have a hotel room here in town?" I nervously stuck the keys in my pocket.

Max shook his head. "It's not a problem though."

Grabbing the two backpacks out of the Jeep, I glanced at my yard. "You could use the spare room if you're too tired to drive."

Max shifted his weight on his feet. "I don't think so."

"Okay. Be sure to check yourself over for ticks when you take a shower. That wooded area looked like a tick resort." I still wasn't looking at him. My fingers were playing with the straps on the backpack. I wanted him to stay. Not for sex, although that would have been great, but I truly did miss him. Since I had come back from California, it almost felt like something was missing in my life. Instinctively I knew it was Max that I was missing.

"I will."

"Thanks for your help." I finally looked up. "Don't be a stranger. Call if you ever want to talk."

He said nothing for several seconds then moved to his BMW. He slid in, rolled down the window and looked at me. "See you, Mel."

I moved my hand in a short sort of wave as he pulled away. I waited until he was gone. As I stood there, I swiped at my nose. Then I blew out my breath. No use getting upset over past mistakes. It was over, plain and simple. Maybe we could still be friends though. Still, time to move on with life.

I went inside and grabbed a quick shower after picking six ticks off my body. When I was done, I headed to the back yard with a towel around me. I lit a light on the deck, turned the stereo to a soft rock CD, and slid into the gazebo with my beer. I lifted the lid off the hot tub and turned it on. It was warm but not hot, and I knew that I needed the massage on my muscles and joints. After it was running nicely, I dropped the towel on the bench near the tub and slid in.

Ah! Oh yeah, this is great. I closed my eyes and relaxed. The slight warmth and massaging action was relaxing to my tired and sore joints. As I sat there, I reviewed my agenda for the next day, not wanting my thoughts to return to Max and that situation. Then I just stared up at the stars through the hole in my gazebo. It was a beautiful night.

Suddenly my attention riveted on a noise in my back yard. A car door had closed quietly, not the usual slamming from my tenants. I sat up in the hot tub and listened. Sure enough my gate creaked. I could only make out a shape in the dark.

The foot steps were light and they hesitated then moved toward the gazebo. I looked at the towel and was just moving toward it, when the shape appeared at the deck.

"Mel?"

I gave out a huge sigh of air. "You scared me!"

Max moved into the gazebo and looked down. His eyes looked at the towel on the bench. His eyes met mine.

"Yes?"

Max pulled his hand from behind his back. In it was a six pack. "I brought beer."

I laughed.

Max's eyes strayed down in the tub then he quickly returned his eyes to mine. "I remembered what Grandma told me when she was in California, and she reminded me again last night. Life is a bumpy road. Hitting some pot holes along the way only makes the smooth highways that much nicer."

"What does that mean?"

"I don't know, but I really didn't want to spend the night in some podunk hotel room." Max smiled. He sat down on the bench. "I thought I'd share a drink with a friend instead."

My heart beat faster and a ray of hope brightened my night. *Maybe it isn't over.* I looked at him in the moonlight. With a big swig, I finished off my bottle. I sat it on the side of the tub and held out my hand for another.

Max handed it to me with a sexy look. "I like the natural look, Mel."

I smirked. I took a drink and spit it out. "It's warm!"

Max laughed. "Yeah. I just bought it but with this heat…."

"Still can't treat a girl right, huh Bauer?" I smiled. "Put them in the fridge and grab two cold ones." I pointed at the French doors that led into the house.

Max disappeared inside then reappeared bottle in hand. He once more sat on the bench after handing me the bottle.

"Where's your beer?"

"What I really want is to take a shower."

I motioned to the house. "Towels are in the hall closet."

Max nodded and headed inside again.

I smiled, sitting there drinking. *Yep. Maybe I still have a chance with him. Maybe he is still interested.* I didn't move one inch from the tub but sat back and relaxed again. It wasn't long, and I heard movement in the kitchen. Max joined me in the gazebo again, this time holding two beer bottles in one hand.

"Need a refill?"

"Are you playing waiter?"

Max chuckled. "Depends. Are you a big tipper?" He was referring to our first conversation ever, when I had been a waitress in my dad's bar.

My eyes met his. "I could be."

He handed me one. My eyes swept over his body taking in the fact that he was only dressed in a towel wrapped around his hips. And it was low on his hips, showing off his swimmer abs. His chest was even more cut than before. My eyes drifted down then back up to met his eyes.

I scooted over in the hot tub.

With a quick flip of his hand, the towel fell off and he slid into the tub. He got comfortable then looked up through the hole in the gazebo.

"The last storm we had put a branch through the roof. I was going to have it patched, but I kind of like it that way." I pointed toward the sky.

"Nice," Max said then closed his eyes. "Despite the heat, this feels good."

I didn't answer, just sat watching him. We sat that way in silence drinking the beers for quite a while.

After some time Max sat up and opened his eyes.

"So, what have you been doing?"

"Traveling. I hated it as a kid, but it's better now. I get to do and see more things. Grandma has three houses in the States and two in Europe. She's thinking of buying another in Italy, so she is always on the move."

"She seems really attached to you."

Max nodded and finished his beer. "Mrs. Lin and Grandma were around more when I was growing up than my parents." He paused. "I'm closer to her than my mom."

"You never answered my question earlier. Is there any one in your life now?"

Again Max studied me before answering. "No. I turned down a marriage proposal last week, but no, I'm not dating anyone right now." He paused. "You?"

I shook my head. "I've been asked out. Won't go."

"Why?"

I shrugged. "None of them felt right."

Max looked away from me. He set his bottle on the side of the tub. "Does the offer of a room still stand?"

I looked at him as I finished my bottle. I waited until I swallowed to answer. "Of course."

Max didn't answer but slowly leaned closer to me. "Good," he whispered in my ear.

My heart was beginning to beat fast again. The heat in my body, not from the hot tub, was settling in all the familiar places.

Max kissed me on the cheek, a 'kissing cousin' kind of kiss. "See you in the morning." With that, he stood up and grabbed his towel. He quickly placed it on his hips and grabbed his empty bottle.

I was stunned and shocked. I wanted a kiss. And possibly more. "Max?"

He turned and looked me in the eye. His eyes were simmering blue in the moonlight. "Like you wanted in California, we're just friends." He paused to let that sink in. "Thanks for the spare room." Then he disappeared into the house.

I just sat there. All of my senses were reeling. Then I grimaced. *He did that on purpose!* I could feel anger rising fast. Then I stopped myself. *It's only fair. I hurt him. I don't like it, but it's what I asked for. Don't get mad.* Disappointment settled deep in my bones. *Friends. It's a beginning. I can start over.*

I waited for sometime before getting up. After shutting everything down, I headed to my bedroom. As I passed the spare room, I glanced in to see him already asleep. At least it looked that way. I sighed softly, continued to my room and climbed into bed.

***

Around noon I pulled into my lot to find Max, dressed in khaki shorts and a cream colored polo shirt, leaning on his car talking on his cell phone. I hopped out of my Jeep as he was hanging up. "Sleep well?"

"Excellent. I like that bed, just firm enough but not too hard." His eyes were amused. "I was getting ready to get something to eat. Are you home for lunch?"

I grabbed a file out of the passenger seat. "Yeah. Took the rest of the day off, more or less. Later, I'm heading to the farm to talk to the renter." I looked at him. "Staying for lunch or what?"

"I guess I can."

I headed into the house with Max following. "So…" I turned to looked at him as he closed the French door from the deck. "How long are you staying in town?"

Max shrugged.

Our eyes met. I narrowed mine. *Is he playing a game? A head game?* I was never good at dating head games. I preferred straight out honesty. He smiled. "I have left over pizza or sandwich stuff. What's your pleasure?"

"I ate the pizza for breakfast." Max grinned bigger. "Guess it's sandwich stuff."

"I guess so." I pulled out the meat and he got glasses. We sat and started eating.

Max dug into his pocket and placed a key on the table in front of me. It was the one I had left with a note on the table when I left this morning while he was sleeping. "Here."

I looked at the key for a few seconds then back at him. "You can stay here for the duration, if you want."

"I can afford a hotel room. Now that I'm in the family good graces again, I have more money than I know what to do with, to be honest."

I shrugged. "The offer still stands." I purposely didn't touch the key but continued eating.

"I'll think about it."

"So, what are you going to do while you're here? It's not like we have that much to see… except corn fields."

Max laughed, knowing that I had been implying a statement he made long ago. "True." He wiped his hands on his napkin and sat back. "I'm going out with a couple of guys from the force tonight."

I took another bite of sandwich as I watched him.

"Did you find out anything about the skeleton yet?"

"Yep. It's an old grave like we thought. The state Medical Examiner thinks it's at least 100 years old. The full autopsy isn't in yet. Also it's an adult male, he thinks. The final report will be in in a couple of weeks, since it's definitely not Carmen." I paused briefly. "I also tried calling that former manager of Griffin Industries—the name you gave me. The phone was busy all morning."

"I know," Max said with a smile. "I was talking to Melvin."

I smirked. "Find out anything?"

"He doesn't remember her too well. He thinks Papios left in the early seventies. The only thing he remembered for sure was that she slept around a lot or at least was rumored to. He never did find out why she was fired, if she was, but he thinks it had to do with one of the bosses and her having a relationship. As to where she went, he had no clue."

"Hmmm."

"But…"

"But?"

Max's face broke into the widest smile. "He did give me a number of the possible boss who she might have had a relationship with. Herman Harnandez now lives in Pennsylvania. I have a call into him."

I frowned.

"What?"

"Are you doing this to get back at me for working your case when you were here?"

Max laughed. "Mel, you do make my day. No. I just had access and thought I would help."

"You know this is helping Bart."

Max nodded. "I talked to John last night for a few minutes while you busy. I think it'd be funny for him to learn that he's a bastard child or out of wedlock. Not that it matters much now days. It'd serve him right."

I shook my head.

"Is he still pursuing you?"

"Yes and no. He doesn't ask any more for me to spend the night with him. But he's still hitting on me when we're together when no one's around, like at the charity thing. And I know for a fact he still intends to bed me."

Max's eyes got hard. "How?"

"He told me so."

"He just came out and told you?"

I nodded as I finished my soda. "Yep. Right before the charity ball. John had just left to check in with some people. Bart pushed me up against the wall and held me there, looking into my eyes. He said, 'Mel, I am going to do you someday. And it'll be the best you've ever had. Maybe not today, maybe not tomorrow, but I will have you.'"

Max scowled. He leaned forward. "You know he was arrested for rape once?"

"I know. Got off on a technicality."

"And this doesn't worry you?"

"What can I do? He's not actually stalking me. He's not making any threats. He just promised that he'd do me. I don't feel overly threatened."

"And if he corners you some night or something somewhere?" The blue eyes were steel now.

"What do you want me to say?" I tossed the rest of my sandwich on the table. "I've done everything to make him understand. If it comes down to me being raped, then I'll probably fake it and just let him make love to me. At least that way, he won't hurt me."

Max sat back still mad. He was breathing a lot faster than before. His hand was slightly clenched. "I don't like it."

"Neither do I."

"Do John and Rich know?"

"Sort of. I told John after the charity ball. I don't want Rich to know."

"What did John say?"

"Watch my step. Keep him informed and keep records of all of the conversations with Hessor."

Max stood up and walked to the counter. He looked out the kitchen window into the back yard. Finally he turned and leaned on the counter. "Do you think he'll follow through on his threat?"

I considered. "Maybe. I think it's sort of a game to him. He has a steady lover, so it's not like he's not getting any." I looked up at Max. "Still, he's tried it before."

"He tried to rape you before?" Max was tense all over; not one part of his body was relaxed.

"Sort of. More of date rape or attempted date rape. When we were teens. He and I went across the shoot from Eleven Bottoms. Remember the fishing camp where I found Scott Hiccome's body?"

Max nodded.

"When we got on the other side, he proposed we go skinny dipping. I didn't answer and he stripped. Then when I just stood there, he grabbed me and we began wrestling. At first I thought he was playing, but I realized he was serious. I relaxed, he made his move, I kicked him in the family jewels. While he laid there in pain, I got in the boat and rowed back to the camp. I didn't see him again until that night at O'Reilly's when you saw us. Remember?"

"Yeah."

"Later when I talked to him at his house, he told me that we could have a replay of that night. And that he would win this time. So, I'm not sure if he's serious or not."

Max rubbed his beard in thought. Suddenly his head snapped up. "Hessor was your source for that information on Mouse, wasn't he?"

I laughed. "Is that still bothering you? Yes, he was." I had used Bart for information on the first case with Rich. It was while I was battling over territory with Max, and he tried hard to find out who my source was.

Max rolled his eyes. "If you had told us that then, it would have saved us a lot of time."

I shrugged as I looked at my watch. "I gotta get going."

"Where?"

"The gym. I'm still working on my chest muscles." I gathered up the leftovers and began putting them away. "Then I'm going back out to the farm."

"I thought the renter didn't get off work until after five?"

"True. I looked up the actual plat of the property. There is another house on the land. Abandoned. Rich mentioned that it was deserted. He checked it out briefly the other night. Said he peeked in the windows. Rich's description about where it is was rather vague. I'm going to try to find it."

"So you think Carson buried his daughter there?"

"No. Kevin's dogs would have found a dead body, besides I think she's still alive. And I think that Carson is living on the farm. He was a hunter and an avid outdoors man. It wouldn't surprise me if he isn't living in the woods on the farm. I want to find him."

Max stopped gathering the glasses. "Why are you so taken in by this, Mel?"

"I just want to find him. And the girl. I want to prove to myself I was right," I said without looking at Max. I set the dishes on the counter near the sink.

Max grabbed my arm and turned me around. "You got that pit bull look about you. Why?"

I looked him in the eyes. "The father molested her. That's why they got a divorce and he lost all visitation rights. He took her from her family."

Max said nothing but didn't let go of my arm either.

"She's only eight."

His eyes were burning into mine. His blue eyes seemed endless in their depth.

"She has her whole life ahead of her. She deserves a chance of living it."

"You're obsessed with this."

"As long as the bastard might be in my neck of the woods, I want to find him."

"And if she is dead?"

"Then at least her mom and family can grieve."

Max let go of my arm, but his eyes were still holding mine. "This girl is not Robbie. You might not be able to save her."

My volcanic anger erupted instantly, and I swung on Bauer.

He caught my hand with his and held it. His blue eyes were shining bright in the knowledge that he had figured out my real reason for searching for the girl. Max squeezed my hand and brought it down still holding tight. "You've got to let go of Robbie."

"I have." Tears formed in my eyes.

"Sure." Max slowly released my hand then pulled me into a hug. "So you say." He patted my back then pushed me away. With a quick move, he picked the key up off the table. "As you drive to the gym, tell me the facts you have on this girl."

"Why?"

"I want to help." He walked out the back door.

I stood there for a second, then grabbed my exercise bag and locked up. Max was already in my Jeep waiting. As I climbed in, I handed him the file that I'd brought home.

He took it with a glance. Then he smiled. "Your anger management classes didn't work, Tiger."

I snorted and squealed my tires leaving the parking lot.

***

Max was still reading the file as he sat in the lobby of the gym. He glanced up at me as I exited the secured area of the gym. I was dressed back in jeans and t-shirt. I had debated wearing shorts but opted for long pants, because I figured we'd encounter lots of brush as we tried to find the old house, if it even existed.

I tossed my bag into the back of the Jeep and hopped in. The small bikini top wasn't making much shade as the sun beat down on us. I glanced at Max, but he was once more reading the file on the girl.

"Interesting reading?

"Did anyone investigate the other members of Carmine's family?"

"New Jersey State Police and the Police in Trenton. Rich talked to them. They're positive that Brady took her."

Max nodded as I pulled into traffic. He closed the file. "I still don't see why they think he's here."

"They, the police don't. They, the private investigator that the family hired does, or at least it's one possibility."

75

"I saw that. He used to rent the farm from Mrs. Crabtree, but that's still a long shot that he's here. He hasn't lived here in over ten years."

"So? Maybe he really liked it." I glanced at Max as I drove. "You only lived here a couple of months and yet you're back."

"That's different."

"Not really. He doesn't have any relatives here…" I drifted off in thought.

"What?" Max stared a me as we sat at the stop light.

"Oh, man! How dumb can we be?" I checked traffic beside and behind me. Since no one was in it or coming, I switched lanes and made a right turn.

Max had to grab the side of the Jeep at my fast maneuver. "What the…?"

"What if he had a girl friend?" I shook my head. "We've been so stupid."

Max seemed to be thinking hard. "Where are we off to? And how are you going to find out who his girlfriend was, if he had one, ten years ago?" His tone was skeptical.

"The office and then the farm," I said as I accelerated a little over the speed limit. I ignored his second question.

"Mel, slow down!"

I merely smiled.

It wasn't long and I was seated at my desk. Max was talking with John in his office. The door was closed. I wondered about that but let it go. I needed to concentrate on my thoughts. As I booted up the computer, I picked up the phone. "Beth, I have a question for you." Beth Majoram was one of my closest friends and also she was hooked into the grapevine of the city. She knew more about people than most people realized, maybe even more than she realized. She was a great source of information.

"Shoot."

"Brady Carson. Ever heard of him?"

There was a silence while she thought. "No. Should I have?"

"Probably not." I quickly relayed the information about the case. "How would I go about finding out if he had a girlfriend here ten years ago?"

"Wow. You aren't asking much, are you?"

I chuckled. "Come on, Beth. Which ladies are the biggest gossips in town?"

Another silence on the phone as she thought. "That's a hard one. I don't think the gossips in town could help. Let me call my mother-in-law out in Breyerton. Maybe she might know someone that lived nearer the farm that might be gossipy. But don't count on much, Mel."

I smiled at the phone. Now that Beth was on the hunt, it wouldn't take long to find out. Talk about me being a bit bull.

We said goodbye. Next on my agenda was searching the data base for more on where he might have worked. I started typing, then stopped suddenly. We knew that Brady had been arrested once while in town on a charge of drunken, disorderly behavior. *Who had bailed him out?* It hadn't been in Rich's notes, and Rich was out with his phone turned off.

I dialed another number. "Mitch Addison, please… Thanks."

As I waited, Max walked into the office and sat down in front of the desk. "This desk is much better than your old one." He was referring to the fact that it took John and Rich almost four months to get me a desk. Before, I had been using the conference room table.

"Funny."

"So, who was Carson dating?"

"I don't know yet. I'm working on it."

Max glanced at his watch. "It's been ten minutes and you don't know?"

I smirked. "Miracles take twenty minutes."

Max laughed.

John stuck his head into the office. "I'm out of here. Good thought, Mel. Keep on it. Let Rich know. Max says that you're headed to the farm again."

I nodded.

John almost smiled. "If you find any more bodies, call me."

I flipped him off and listened as he chuckled down the hall.

"Addison."

"Mitch, yeah… How can I find out who bailed someone out ten years ago?"

"The old arrest file would have it, as would the court house. Who and why?"

"Is that public record?"

"Yeah. Might take a while to find it though. Why?"

Max got comfortable in his chair.

"Really! Cool. Thanks. Talk at you later." I hung up the phone and stood up. "Coming?" I asked Max as I passed him.

He immediately moved out of the chair and followed me down the hall to the front entrance. "Where?"

I passed Pam at the desk. "I'm in a hurry. Could you shut down my computer?"

"Sure," Pam said with a smile and a glance at Max. "Hey, Mel... Your messages." She held out a piece of paper. "He called while you were on the phone."

I back tracked and took the message. It was from Bart. "Call him back. Tell him John will call him as soon as he can." I walked out the door.

"Who was it from?" Max asked catching up with me on the sidewalk.

"Bart."

Max looked puzzled as we walked down the street to my Jeep.

"He's supposed to work though John, not me." I hopped in and motioned for Bauer to get a move on. "Come on. Are you getting slow in your leisure time?"

"Tenacious little witch, aren't you?" he said as he jumped in.

I barely waited for him to get buckled and took off.

"Where to? I don't think I caught it the first time." The sarcasm was as thick as the humidity.

"The court house. Mitch said that if they were still on file..." I glanced at Max then realized he didn't have a clue what I was talking about. "Brady was bailed out on a drunken disorderly charge by someone ten years ago. By who? The court house will still have it on file, if they still have the records. Otherwise it'll take more time to research. Maybe we'll get lucky and the records will be right there."

"They will."

"Why do you say that?"

78

"Because you are lucky." Max smiled.

I smiled back. "Let's hope."

***

But I wasn't lucky. The only thing they had on record was the name of the bail bondsman. And a quick look at the phone book revealed that he was no longer in business. I tried Rich, but he still wasn't answering his phone. John was also out of touch. I called a bail bondsman that I met through Mitch, but he didn't know anything either.

I sat in the Jeep thinking. *How do I find out about this bail bondsman?*

Max just watched me.

I suddenly nodded to myself. It was a long shot, but I was willing to try anything at this point. I started the Jeep and once more hurried away from the curb.

"Slow down, Mel," Max exclaimed. He shook his head. "Maybe I ought to drive from now on. Do you want to get a ticket or what?"

I just smiled. Only a short two minutes later I was pulling up to a brick two story house in a decrepit part of town. The house had seen better days. It had at one time been a single family home, maybe in the thirties or forties, but now it and the others around it had been converted to multifamily housing and over the years had been left to neglect.

I hesitated with a look at Max. I could ask him to wait in the car, but I knew that was useless. "Let me do the talking, okay?"

"You're the boss." He inclined his head as he got out.

I huffed as we walked up to the door. I knocked loudly. It took a while, but finally it was answered. Just like the last time I had been here, the door only opened to it's chain. The lady was again smoking a cigarette.

"Yeah?"

"Hi. I'm Mel Addison. Is Tooney home?"

She looked me up and down, then stared at Max. "You've been here before."

"Last year about this time."

"I remember you." She puffed again looking at Max. "Who are you?"

"This is Max Bauer," I answered. "He's with me."

"A cop?"

"No way. He works with me."

The lady considered. "He looks like a cop."

I laughed. "Yeah, I know. We use that to our advantage at times. He's not a cop."

"Tooney said last time that you were okay." She coughed. "He's around back." She thumbed to the side of her house and closed the door.

"Thanks," I said as it closed and made a motion for Max to move off the porch.

"You lie well," Max said in a whisper as we moved to the still broken down gate.

"I didn't lie. You aren't a cop. You're working with me, and we might still use it to our advantage." I grinned evilly and opened the gate. I swallowed a large lump down my throat and hacked silently.

"Who is this guy?"

"An old drug dealer who knew Dad and Rich. If it was happening back then, he knew about it." I stepped over several broken chairs and yard stuff.

Max followed slowly.

I headed directly to a patch of green garden in the otherwise brown yard. "Tooney?" I called to the man of around late sixties working a hoe.

He looked up. "Well, if it isn't little Mel." His eyes focused on Max then came back to me. He stood up and leaned on his hoe.

I pointed to the shaded area where there were two chairs. It was under a large tree which looked deader than before. The number of living limbs with leaves had diminished. "Can we talk?"

He again eyed Max, then with a nod, set the hoe down in the dirt. Tooney walked slowly to the chairs. He once more looked Max up and down.

"Tooney, this is Max Bauer. He's working with me on a case. I need some information about something from about ten years ago."

Tooney motioned to sit.

Max shook his head. "Go ahead. I'll stand."

"No offence, Mr. Bauer, but you look like a cop."

"You know, I get that all the time. It was even worse when I didn't have a beard," Max said, scratching his chin. "Or it might have been because I was a cop at one point."

Tooney glanced at me. "Where?"

"Here in town for a couple of months. And in California for about ten years. Is that a problem for you?" Max stuck his hands in his pockets.

Tooney just looked at me.

"I'll vouch for him Tooney; he may be a jerk at times, but he's helping me with a case." I got comfortable and smiled at Max's dirty look. "I'm trying to find a guy that kidnapped his daughter and molested her. That was in New Jersey. We think he's back here in town. He lived here for a short time, at the Crabtree farm for a year or so."

Tooney got comfortable. He glanced up at Max who was relaxed with hands still in his pockets. The older man turned his attention back to me.

"His name is Brady Carson. He was bailed out ten years ago by Herdsman Bail Bonds on a drunken disorderly charge. I want to find out who bailed him out, but no one remembers the business." I scratched my head. "My next stop is the library to go through the old micro fiche phone books, but if I don't have to go that route, I don't want to."

Tooney nodded. "I knew Al."

"Good. Is he still alive?"

"If you call it living. He's in Good Sam."

"How's his memory?"

Tooney held up his hand and wiggled it back and forth. "So, so."

"Might he remember?"

"I doubt it. A drunken disorderly charge?" Tooney shook his head. "That's nickel and dime. A bigger charge maybe, and maybe five years ago he might remember, but now." Tooney made a noise in his throat.

I sighed. It had been a long shot after all.

"The one you want to talk to is his secretary."

I glanced up at Max who raised his eyebrows in surprise. "Yeah?"

Tooney nodded. "You wouldn't by any chance have a smoke on you would you?" He glanced up at the house.

"Sorry. Neither of us smoke."

"I have to quit and the nag inside watches like a hawk." He ran a hand through his thin grey hair. "Where was I?"

"Al Herdsman's secretary," I reminded him.

"Oh yeah. Marsha or Marris…" He seemed to be thinking hard. He stood up. "Let me ask the nag, she'll know." He walked to the house and disappeared inside.

Max looked around the yard. "What did he do?"

"The major drug dealer in town before the Hessors."

"And he lives here? So he wasn't very good at it?"

"Don't speak bad about him." I winked. "Dad says he only lives here part of the time. He also owns a house in Florida and one in Washington State. According to Dad, this is where he comes during the spring and summer for some reason. And I've been told by sources that the inside of the house is beautiful. This is a cultivated look."

"Really?" He looked around again, then we lapsed into silence for a few minutes.

Suddenly I slapped my head, "Duh!"

Max grinned. "What?"

"Dad would probably know the bail bondsman. Why didn't I think of him?"

Tooney walked out the door. He was muttering to himself. "I called Marris Cletonski." He sat down and handed me a slip of paper with an address on it. "She's expecting you."

I stood up and kissed Tooney on the cheek. "Thanks. If I can ever do anything for you, let me know."

Tooney stood up and chuckled. "You just did." He did a little dance. "Hoochie momma."

I laughed, along with Max, as we walked out of the back yard.

"Tell Dickie I want a free drink next time I'm in his bar," Tooney called to me as he moved back to his hoe.

"I'll tell Dad that it's on me," I called back as the gate closed.

Max waited until we had pulled away from the curb before asking, "What is Good Sam?"

"Good Samaritan Home. A nursing home in town. If you're going to help me, you've got to learn the lingo."

"Oh yeah, I'll put that tops on my list of things to do, learn Quincy lingo. As long as I have my personal translator along, I don't need to."

"And what if you visit here, and I'm long gone?" I smirked.

"I think I would be able to suffer through it." He smirked back.

***

"Well, Tooney said you were looking into a child kidnapping and…" The sixty-something lady with grey hair looked at me as we sat on the couch in her living room. "Addison? Any relation to Dickie?"

"His youngest daughter."

Marris chuckled. "Dickie was a character. Okay, so what was the low life's name again?"

"Brady Carson. He was bailed out on a drunken disorderly charge ten years ago." I pulled out my copy of the record from city hall and handed it to her. "I realize that this is really stretching it…"

"Hmmm. Do you have a picture of him?"

Max spoke, "There's one in the file that's out in the car, Mel. I'll get it." Shortly he handed her a picture of Brady that we had gotten from New Jersey.

"Yep. I do remember him. He hit on me. He was real flirty and said some nasty things." She blushed. "Not many guys did that back then. I was already older than the hills."

We both smiled.

"Do you by any chance remember who bailed him out?"

Marris closed her eyes and thought back. "I used to have a really good memory but age and all…" Finally she shook her head. "I remember it was a woman, but other than that, no. Sorry."

"Well, thanks for trying." I handed her my card. "If you think of anything else call me."

"Sorry I couldn't help."

"That's okay. It was a long shot. At least you confirmed it was a woman."

We walked to the car and Max patted my arm. "It was a good try."

"Yeah." I sighed. "Out to the farm." I started up the Jeep.

"Out to the farm," Max repeated.

***

It took a little bit of work, but we finally found the dirt road that might lead to the old, abandoned house on the property. The road was nearly covered by small trees and over-growth; we almost missed the turn off.

"Someone has used this recently," I said to Max with a quick glance. Some of the larger small trees had been knocked down—others had been bent over. And there were very faint tire tracks still in the grass.

"Yeah, I noticed." He was looking around. He stood up in the Jeep and looked farther ahead. We had taken the bikini top off when we reached the woods. "Slow down, Mel. Looks like there's a clearing ahead. Probably the old house area. Let's approach on foot."

I brought the Jeep to a stand-still. After shutting it off we waited, listening—nothing but crickets and wood noises.

Max hopped out and looked around. "Let's not approach from the road." He pointed at the woods.

"Yeah, let's see if someone is there first." We headed into the woods and paralleled the 'road.' Sure enough, soon we could see a dilapidated house in a sort of clearing. It was clearly abandoned. All of the glass had been broken out, and the grass was over knee high. The only area that wasn't swimming in weeds and grass was a large dirt area immediately surrounding the house. The trees made a nice circle around the house, giving less than half an acre of 'house area.' We could see huge piles of something, maybe brush and old dead trees, on the opposite side of the clearing.

We stopped before leaving the woods, checking out the area first. I pointed to the back of the house. "Is that some sort of vehicle?" I whispered.

Max nodded. "But is it abandoned too? It looks really rusty, even from here." His eyes were taking in the house again. "Let's approach from this side."

84

"Good idea. No windows." I smiled. One side of the house was completely lacking windows. I moved quietly though the woods, picking my way between trees. Max followed on my heels. We stopped again on the edge of the woods, checking things out.

"You're good at the quiet stuff," Max whispered.

His breath on my ear gave me shivers up and down my spine, causing my heart to beat faster and heat to settle in. "I played a lot of Cowboys and Indians with my brothers. I was always an Indian."

Max chuckled softly.

I flicked my head to the house and we left the woods behind us. It was a good fifty feet from the woods through tall grass, weeds, and low young trees to the house.

When we got to the house, Max motioned for me to take the front while he checked the back and abandoned vehicle. I nodded and moved to the front corner. I glanced back to see him looking around his corner. He glanced back at me, and I gave him a thumbs up. I could tell Max chuckled before disappearing from view.

I moved to the front of the house, stopping once to peek into a busted out window. As expected, abandoned. I moved away from the window and looked around the area. *Why did I feel like I was being watched?* I couldn't see anyone, so I looked into the window on the other side of the door. Nothing. Giving one last look around again, I pushed on the door that hung half off of one hinge.

Before actually stepping inside the house, I checked it out. The floor was falling apart. The door frame looked sturdy, but there were floor boards missing and others were broken. I went to move into the house when I heard movement from the far side. I froze.

Max walked around the corner. "It was an abandoned tractor. I doubt anyone has been here in awhile." He looked around too.

"Yeah. I'm going to check out the house anyway."

Max nodded. "Be careful. It looks unsafe."

I stepped into the interior and noticed the smell first. A slight odor of something. I turned up my nose. *What is that smell? It doesn't smell like dead body, but I've smelled it before.* I couldn't put my finger on it. I cautiously picked my way around the bottom floor; nothing except for piles of debris. I did see some food wrappers. I turned one over.

They weren't too old, maybe only a couple of weeks. I recognized the candy wrappers from the candy bars I had handed out to the teens. It was a new contest the company was sponsoring. So, someone had been here. It wouldn't surprise me if teens were using it as a make out place or a place to do drugs.

I moved into what looked to have been the living room and checked it out. Okay, someone had been here recently. There was a scorched area off to the side where a fire had been made. I wandered over to the stairs.

I squatted down and looked closely at them. There were footprints in the dust. They looked large, like a man's boot. I looked farther up a couple more steps and saw a smaller foot print. A child's barefoot print.

I slowly followed the prints up the stairs, being careful to stay near the other prints. Parts of the stairs looked bad. When I got to the top, I glanced around. Not much different from downstairs. I followed the foot prints to a room. This was the best looking room in the place. I stopped at the doorway.

It was clean. Someone had been here and very recently. I gingerly moved around the room, avoiding a huge hole in the floor. I peeked down the hole, and my gut clenched. It was directly over the place where the fire had been. Moving away from the hole, I took a more detailed look at the room. One of the windows had been boarded up, but sunlight poured thru the other window.

Wallpaper was peeling off the walls in most places or was completely off. The room didn't smell musty like the bottom floor or have that other smell. My eyes scanned the length of the room and for the first time noticed a small piece of metal near the base board of one wall, right under the boarded up window. It was a newly installed eye bolt. I squatted down by it and noticed the floor had been scuffed up around the eye bolt. It reminded me of the pattern of wood that was on Beth's dog kennel where they occasionally chained up their dog.

Someone or something had been chained up in the room. I stood and moved to the door. As I descended the steps, I screwed up my face at the smell again. *What is that?* Finally, it hit me as I exited the stairs.

That was the same sort of smell I smelled from those portable johns. Human excrement.

"Max!" I called out as I moved through the front door. I stepped out to see a strange sight. Max was picking himself up off the ground. Very slowly. He almost lost his balance at one point.

I froze. "Max?!"

Then I heard a noise. A car engine. Racing. And coming closer. My head swiveled in the direction. A large truck was headed directly at Max. And Max had not a clue it was headed his way.

I gasped, glanced his way, then back at the truck. With a surge of adrenaline, I took off running toward Max, not more than fifteen yards away, yelling. I saw the truck racing toward him at the same time. My heart pounded. There was no way I was going to be able to beat the truck to Max.

I flung myself at Max, grabbing him by the shirt, knocking him down and away from the path of the truck. It barely missed us. We rolled over and over in the tall grass. Finally we came to rest with Max on top of me.

I couldn't breathe. My eyes were open, but I couldn't see anything. The sun blinded me. A crushing weight was on me, stopping my breath. I heard noise.

A scraping sound. Cutting. And voices. Yelling. Yelling in panic to move faster. More cutting noises. Metal on metal.

"Breathe."

I heard a voice call to me. I tried breathing. Pain. I opened my mouth to speak but nothing came out.

"Mel, breathe!"

"Out!" I screamed. At least that was what I was thinking. "Out. I want out." I know I took a breath at that point, because it hurt, but the pressure was no longer on me. Thank God!

I took another breath. "Out. I want out."

"Out of what? Just breathe, Mel. Breathe."

My hands were free, and I started moving them. I could finally move and now breathing was easier. I blinked, and the light seemed to have moved because it was no longer in my eyes. I blinked again and saw Max looking down at me. I took a deep breath. *Max? What was going on?* I sat up and looked around.

"You scared the hell out of me." Max sat down holding his head.

I glanced around the area. *Woods. Woods?* Suddenly my brain kicked in. *The truck. Someone had tried to run Max over.* I jumped up and fell right back down. My legs shook. I looked at my hands, and they were shaking too. I rubbed them together, then I rubbed my legs. I needed to get the circulation back. It felt like they had been asleep from being trapped. But...

"Mel, talk to me... Mel?"

"I'm okay. I'm okay. I'm okay." I stood back up. I brushed off my pants then opened and closed my hands, staring at them.

Max was now standing next to me. "Talk to me Tiger."

"I'm okay. I'm out. I'm okay." I was still staring at my hands. *No blood. I was okay.* Suddenly I was being shaken. I looked at the guy shaking me.

"Mel!"

"Yeah?" I shook my head. "Come on. We need to find out where he went but... I'm out. Yeah, it's okay. I'm out. He's gone, I think." I began walking. I heard walking behind me. As we reached the edge of the woods, I was turned around forcibly.

"Stop. You aren't making sense."

I blinked, finally seeing Max. Then I noticed that he had blood running down his face. "Are you okay?" I gently moved his hair to the side and saw the cut, a gash in his scalp. "Max, we need to get you to the hospital. You're going to need stitches." I grabbed the head band that I sometimes wear in my exercise class and placed it on his head over the cut.

"Mel...." Max once more grabbed my arm. "Talk to me a minute."

"How is your vision?"

"Mel, stop and look at me." Max took his hand and brought my face close so he could look me in the eyes. "Take a deep breath."

I did.

"Calm down."

I took another breath. My heart was slowly returning to its normal rhythm.

"What just happened?"

"A truck tried to run you over." I almost smiled. "We need to get going. It had to be Brady. I found evidence that someone has been living in the house. I was coming out to tell you when I saw you picking yourself up off the ground. Then the truck."

Max nodded and let go of my face. "Yes, I know that. And I thank you for saving my life. But that's not what I meant. What was that after the truck? All of that 'out' stuff?"

"What?… Uh, I was… I was just stunned. Come on, Max. You need to be seen by a doctor."

We started walking toward the Jeep parked a short way down the road."Does it hurt?" I asked as he grimaced again.

"Yeah. I was walking away from the house and out of nowhere, I get hit by something. I think it was a board. The next thing I know, I'm rolling over and over. Then I looked down to see you white faced and not breathing. You scared the hell out of me. You weren't breathing." He blew out his breath and put his hand to his head. As he wiped the blood off his face, he looked at me.

"I uh, I was stunned by your weight." I looked back at the way we had come. "I need to call John and Rich. Someone was mighty upset that we were here." I dug out my cell phone and placed the call as we walked.

By the time I finished talking to John, we were at the Jeep. I helped Max into the passenger side of the car. He was looking at me in a strange way. I ignored his look and hurried to the other side. After turning the Jeep around, I headed directly to the hospital.

Chapter 8

I got Max settled into the lazy boy in the living room after he was released from the hospital emergency room. I handed him a soda as he got comfortable, then sat on the couch looking at my hands.

"Mel?"

I looked up. "Yeah?'

"What do you remember from the truck? John will be here in a few minutes, and he'll want to know."

I thought about it. My mind was blank. I remember the truck heading toward Max but that was all. I couldn't even clearly see the truck to be honest. "I don't know."

"Come on, Mel. What color was it?"

"I don't know."

"Was it Brady?"

"I don't know."

Max gave me a strange look then made a face. "Look at me. You have a better memory than this. What color was the truck?"

"I don't know!" My heart was beating fast again. It felt hard to catch my breath.

"But…" Max began.

I jumped up, heading directly for the phone in the kitchen. I dialed a number without thinking and waited.

"Yes?" A man's voice. Calm.

"It's me. I need to see you." I glanced at my watch. It was late afternoon. "It's real important. Are you busy?"

There was a slight pause.

"Meet me at home. I'll be there in five minutes. Drive carefully, Mel," the man's voice said, then the phone died.

I slowly hung up the phone but kept my hand on it. I took another deep breath to calm my once more frazzled nerves. I turned and found Max standing there watching me. "I gotta go somewhere. I'll be back in awhile. Go sit down. The doctor said to take it easy." With that, I left the house.

***

"You'll be okay. It's a normal reaction." The older man of around fifty smiled as he escorted me to my Jeep. He lightly squeezed my arm. We both looked up at the same time to find someone watching us.

Max was leaning on his silver BMW, arms crossed, waiting for our approach into the parking lot behind the house I was just in. His face hardened when he glanced at the guy with me.

We stopped in front of Max. The man's calm voice was reassuring. "Take it easy. You'll be fine. Call me again if you need me." With just a glance at Bauer, he moved back to the house.

Max watched him walk away, then stared at me. His blue eyes were once more hard like at the charity ball. His expression was stone.

"It's not what you think."

He didn't answer.

"What are you doing driving on the painkillers anyway? You should be at home resting."

"I thought you said there was no one in your life?" His voice was low and with a tone of something, maybe hurt.

"Abe?" I pointed back to the house. "He's not… What I mean is… He's…" I looked down and fiddled with the bottom of my T-shirt. I finally looked up at Max after composing myself. "Not here." I headed to my Jeep.

Max caught my arm. "No. Now."

I yanked my arm away. "No. Later." I hopped into my Jeep, and before he could get into his car, I was pulling away.

As I drove, I noticed the BMW following. My cell phone rang. I grabbed it and checked the readout. It was a strange number. "Hello?"

"What is going on?"

"I can't talk about it driving." I hung up on Max and shut off my cell phone.

I got home first and was already opening the gate by the time he pulled up. I walked to the back door to find a note taped to it.

'Call ASAP. Turn your cell on.' I recognized John's handwriting.

I reached into my pocket and turned it back on then dialed his number. I was leaning on the counter when Max walked in. "Hi, John. Sorry."

"I got to your place and both of you were gone. What's up?"

I looked at Max who was standing with hands on hips. He had on his 'I'm really pissed' look and his body was stiff. "I just needed to go get something. Max must have driven himself somewhere."

"You were pretty vague on the description of the truck. Can you describe it better?"

"Yeah. It was green. An older truck, maybe a Chevy. It was beat up and had definitely seen better days. I can't say for sure it was Brady, but it was a man with dark colored hair. And John, there was someone sitting next to him in the truck."

"Carmine?"

"Maybe. It was just a glance."

I saw Max relax a bit but his body posture hadn't. "Look, I gotta go. Where are you?"

"Heading to the farm with Rich to check out the house. We'll call when we get back."

I hung up but didn't look at Max as he stood there waiting. The tension in the room thickened as we stood in silence.

"Now you can remember?"

I nodded and moved to get a glass out of the cabinet. "Are you hungry? It's time for supper."

"Tell me who that guy was and what's going on."

"I could order deli if you want, or pizza." I busied myself with getting drinks.

Max grabbed and turned me around. He took the glasses out of my hands and set them on the counter. Moving in close caused me to be pushed to the counter. "Look at me."

I raised my head a little.

"Look at me."

I did.

"Who was that guy?"

"Abraham Geisser." I paused. "My psychiatrist."

Max's jaw dropped just a bit. Finally he sort of shook his head. "A shrink? You said you saw someone, not seeing someone."

"I don't go to regular sessions anymore. Just when I need to." I tried to move away from him, but he took a step to stop me. I studied his wrist watch.

"Why?"

I sighed. He obviously wasn't going to let it go. "I had a flashback. To being trapped in the car." I looked at him as my anger rose. "So? I'm nuts. Now get out of my way." I pushed him aside and stomped out of the kitchen.

I headed to my bedroom. I just wanted to be alone. But Max followed me. I sat on the bed staring at my shoes.

He squatted down. His expression was softer now. He was no longer mad. Max rested his hands on my knees. "It's okay to see someone, Mel. I was just shocked that you were."

I didn't say anything.

Max took my chin and lifted my head. "We all have weaknesses. There's no shame in needing help for a problem."

"Not me."

"Yes, you." Max sat next to me on the bed. He pulled me into a hug. "I'm proud of you to go see a doctor. That takes guts, to admit you have a problem and do something about it."

I leaned into him. It was nice having his arm around me again, even though I knew it wouldn't last. I wanted at least this, for as long as he wanted to hold me.

"How long have you been going?"

"Since I left California. I wasn't sleeping. Nightmares from Devon chasing me. The night he shot me. Flashbacks to being stuck in the car. The pain." My hands trembled.

"That's what you meant when you said you wanted out, huh?"

"I wasn't at the farm but in the car with Craig and Robbie. I could hear the fireman cutting the metal again." My heart beat picked up again, and I took a shallow breath. "I could hear them yelling to each other and working frantically, but I couldn't speak or move. I was conscious most of the time. Worse, I couldn't breathe. My right lung was collapsed. I was impaled by the car on that side." I took a deep, slow breath. "Abe thinks that the weight of you on me brought it back again. He thinks that I…" I drifted off, not wanting to tell Max that Abe thought it was just Max's presence that had brought it on. That I desperately wanted him in my life. I closed my hand to stop the trembling.

"You're okay." He gently rubbed my arm.

"Yeah." I stood up and walked over to my bureau. I touched Robbie's stuffed rabbit. I missed him so much, it was as though I was walking in a fog of sadness.

Max moved to my side. He looked down at the bureau. "Is that Craig and Robbie?" He pointed at a picture of the three of us. It was the only picture I displayed of them. Max had never seen it because I had only put it out when I got back from California.

"Yeah." It was half sigh, half whisper.

Max picked it up for a closer look.

The picture was a posed photo of the three of us just a month before the accident. Robbie was sitting on my lap, and Craig had his arm around me. We looked like a happy family, but the smiles belied the strife going on between Craig and me. I had picked this one, but it was the last photo I had of Robbie.

He set it back down and looked at me. "I think Chinese." He walked out the door and left me standing there.

I didn't move out of the room until Max called to say that supper was here. I moved into the room, surprised to find my favorite Chinese place had delivered.

"But they don't deliver here. I'm too far away from their area."

"Money can buy almost anything." He looked out the window. "Almost anything." Then we ate in silence.

Max finally broke the silence. "I see you've been practicing with the sticks." When Max and I first met, he tried to teach me to eat with chopsticks.

I looked up. "Yeah. It's sort of a game I play with myself. I make myself eat with them for at least ten minutes, then I give up and use a fork. I guess I forgot this time." There was very little left on my plate.

Max's cell phone rang. "Hello?" Then he frowned. "Sophia, I told you no... I'm not where I can talk now."

I motioned for me to leave the room.

Max shook his head. "No, I'm not in Italy. I'm in the States... I said no... Goodbye, Sophia." He hung up.

I lowered my head as I finished off the last bite. My heart was beating fast again, and I didn't look at him. That must have been the lady that proposed. With a quick peek up, I saw that he was staring at me. "What?'

Max smiled. "That is one thing about you."

I looked him in the eye. "What?"

"Never mind." He stood and cleaned up the empty take out boxes. Then pulled his pill bottle out of his pocket and took another one.

I stood and cleaned up the plates and glasses. Then I grabbed my car keys.

"Where are you going?"

"I still need to talk to the renter."

Max stared at me.

"I may be nuts, but I still need to find the girl." I closed my eyes thinking back to the truck. "I can't remember the person next to the driver. Could be a girl. Whoever it was seemed to be cowering in the seat." I opened my eyes. "I don't know, but whoever was driving, didn't like us there. I'm betting it was Brady and Carmine."

"I agree. Let's go."

"Nope. The doc said your stitches need to stay clean and you are to rest."

"So, I won't go rolling about in the dirt or in the woods." Max gave me a slight grin as he touched his head. "This little cut won't stop me from following my favorite snooping sneak." His blue eyes were sparking.

I smiled as I got warm all over. I could accept his friendship and that was enough right now. "Okay, but don't complain about my driving."

"Of course not. Why argue with a nut case?" He punched me in the shoulder as he passed.

"Max. Please don't..."

"I was just kidding, Tiger." He moved back to me. With a light touch, he tapped my nose. "I won't tell anyone."

"Thanks."

"Besides, who would believe me." With a grin, he walked out the door.

***

"I told you, I don't know anything about a man staying in the woods or near that house," the lady said looking at me from behind the screen door.

"I know that." I shifted my weight on my feet and coughed twice. "I just... See, he side-swiped my Jeep as he left." I pointed to the large dent and smear of paint on the side of my car. I hoped she didn't look too hard because the paint was brown not green.

"Yeah? So?"

"I need to find out if he has insurance." I blew out my breath. "Do you know what this will do to my insurance?"

Trisha shrugged with a glance at Max standing off the porch. I glanced with her. Max was looking excessively bored. He was so good at that. I looked back at her.

"I just need a name or something. Have you at least seen him around? Do you know the green truck I'm talking about?"

"Can't say I have." She shifted her weight, then stuck a hand in her pocket. The other hand swiped at her nose for the third time. "I'll keep my eyes open and call you if I do."

I nodded and handed her another card, just in case. "If I can keep this away from the sharks at the insurance agency, I'd like too. But it'll be several hundred dollars to repaint." I sighed in fake anger with a glance at the Jeep.

"If he was driving a beat up truck, I doubt he'll have money to help you. Don't you have uninsured motorist insurance or something like that?" Her hand stuck the card in her pocket. She smoothed her sun dress again.

"I do, but that requires a police report and well, as I told you last time, I've had a few too many run-ins with them lately."

She seemed puzzled. "I thought you worked for an agency in Quincy? Don't you have some sort of working relationship?"

"We do. But see, the cops and I don't always see eye to eye, if you get my meaning. I'm trying to keep my bosses out of it too."

"Why?"

I looked around as though I was worried someone might see or hear me. "Can I be honest with you?"

Her head bobbed. I had her rapt attention.

"My boyfriend and me were looking for a place to party. Those Quincy cops are always following me around. Being a detective and all, I guess they think I'm always on a case or something and they hate us. Anyway, I can't find any good places to, uh, relax. You know what I mean?"

She gave me a puzzled look.

I sighed. "To smoke. You know, to *smoke*. I can't do it in town. If I get caught, it's my license. See. I also don't want this guy reporting me to the cops. Do you know how much fun the Quincy cops would have if the county police told them that they had caught me doing something illegal? So, I guess if he can't help, he can at least not turn me in. I'll figure something out about the accident. I'd appreciate any help you can give me."

The lady's eyes narrowed. "I can't promise, but if I see him, I'll pass it along."

"Great. Thanks. You don't by any chance know of a better place to smoke, do you? That other house is way too decrepit and has too many people going there."

"Good weed?"

"Oh yeah! Max gets it directly from Mexico. Best I've ever had."

She looked closer at Max.

"I bring it right in over the border, through California." Max smiled a big grin. "It's called Mexican Haze."

Trisha glanced around again. "You can get Haze?"

Max put his finger to his lips with a smile.

"Well, that's different. Okay. I'll tell you what, you can smoke here. But it'll cost you two joints."

"Two?" I asked her. "Do you know how much that stuff costs?"

She smiled. "Two joints. And I'll see if I can't find Brady for you."

I looked back at Max. "Can we spare two?"

Max shrugged. "Maybe."

"Let me think about it. Two. Man!" I moved off the porch. "I'll get back to you."

We headed back to the Jeep and took off. Max turned slightly as though looking at me, but he was watching Trisha Bashington. "She's still watching."

I smiled. "Mexican Haze? Is that real?"

"It just started appearing when I quit. I've been told it's really good stuff." He shook his head. "What a line of crap! You lie good."

I laughed. "Bad habits are hard to break."

Max chuckled. "But we know he's in the area and she made a big mistake… We know he communicates with her."

***

I was standing by the kitchen counter doing my morning routine when I heard movement behind me. I glanced, and sure enough Max was walking out dressed only in his baggy shorts that barely hung on his now smaller hips. I swallowed and quickly brought my eyes back up to his face. I didn't need to be having these kinds of thoughts when he only wanted friendship.

"Good morning." He yawned as he stretched almost like a lion.

"Yeah." I glanced at the clock again, reminding myself to remember to take my pills. As I reached for the last of my medicine bottles, I noticed he moved closer to me. "Are you going with me to take over for John?"

After talking with John and Rich about our conversation with Trisha at the farm, we were now doing surveillance at the farm.

"Yeah." He scratched himself as he leaned on the counter. "What's that for?" He pointed at the six pill bottles. Max's eyes changed from guarded blue to a deep ocean blue.

I swallowed the last pills and began gathering the bottles to put them back into the small basket. As I added another one to the basket, he reached over, pulled it out and looked at it. "Do you mind?" I grabbed it back.

"What are the meds for?"

"Me. If you're going with me, you need to get a move on. I need to leave in ten minutes."

"Yeah, okay. The meds? What for? Are you sick?" He moved away from leaning against the counter. "You've been coughing a lot lately."

"That's the only reason I know of that doctors will prescribe medicine." I smirked. Placing the basket back in the small cabinet near the sink, I moved to the fridge.

Max sighed. "I'm going to ask one more time. Why are you taking this much medication?"

"Look, you've made it clear that we're just friends. I don't particularly want to talk about…" My back was to him as I reached for the refrigerator door.

Max swung me around and laid a kiss on my lips. A heart stopping, mouth tingling, shake the earth kind of kiss. His hands were holding my head so I couldn't pull away. It was most definitely a possessive kiss. Finally, he let go. Looking me in the eyes, he spoke just above a whisper, "I love you, you crazy woman. You drive me insane. Are you sick?"

My heart was thumping away in my chest. My loins were tingling with newly aroused passion. I merely stared at him, mouth open, shocked at the sudden turn of events.

With a slight grin, he leaned in this time and kissed me more slowly, this time a very passionate and sensual kiss. He moved, pushing me against the counter without breaking the kiss. His hands were lightly massaging my back and running up and down my arms.

After a moment's hesitation, I leaned into him and gave back as good as he was giving. We started to get worked up. I could feel his need pressed up against mine. We both groaned at the same time.

The phone rang.

I grabbed his head and pressed my body into his. I straddled one on his legs and began to rub on him. I needed this. I wanted this so bad.

The phone continued to ring. Finally after four rings, the answering machine picked up.

Max's hands were beginning to move around to the front. We were kissing hungrily, and he once more moved to hold my head. Just as his hands drifted down past my neck and onto my chest...

"This is Cindy from Dr. Corbet's office..."

I stiffened.

Max responded by stopping the kiss and looking at me.

"...Mel, you need to call the office as soon as possible. Dr. Corbet said..."

I moved out of Max's arms and grabbed the phone. I felt a tightness in my stomach. "Yeah. I'm here."

"Oh hi. This is Cindy. The test results show that you have a bacterial infection in your right lung. You're not contagious, but is has him baffled. He's going to talk to a specialist at John Hopkins in Baltimore. He'll set up an appointment with them if you're good with that."

"Whatever it takes." I stood listening, staring at the floor. My mind went blank from overload. Suddenly I felt my stomach drop. It now felt like my world was a crushing weight. *Oh my God, what is happening to me!*

"Good. In the meantime, he has a couple more meds he would like you to start. He'd also like to see you if possible. Just a quick check. Come in any time, and we'll fit you in. Okay? He said not to worry; he'll get this figured out. I've already called the prescriptions into your pharmacy."

"Okay. Thanks Cindy. I'm busy all day today, but I can stop and talk with him first thing tomorrow morning." I hung up the phone and stood there holding it, my mind reeling with the new information.

"Mel?"

100

I slid down the wall and sat on the floor. I heard, saw, and felt nothing. I laid my head on my knees and bit my trembling lip.

Max sat next to me and pulled me into his embrace. "Talk to me."

I laid my head on his chest. A tear rolled down my face. Shortly, it was followed by others.

Max reached out and caught them with his finger, then kissed me on the cheek. His voice almost broke once. "Is… Is it terminal?"

"We don't know." I looked him in the eye. I sniffled wiping my eyes. "We don't know."

"Tell me." His voice was gentle yet firm.

I sniffled again and wiped my nose on the back of my hand. "My immune system is almost shut down. I… since I came back from your place in California, I have had pneumonia four times. Never enough to hospitalize me but close."

I saw his eyes change. I knew what he was thinking; it showed clearly on his face.

"No. It's not AIDS. I do not have HIV. That was the first thing we checked. I was worried that Craig had contracted something with his affairs. It's not that. But the doctor is sure it has something to do with my lungs and the damage I did. Not to mention the longer than normal recovery from the accident and my ribs after Devon shot me."

Max kissed me on the lips gently and brought me back to his chest. He hugged me so tight it almost hurt.

"I'm very susceptible to colds, viruses and bacteria. When I got back from St. Louis, I felt 'off,' so I went to see Corbet again. I have a bacterial infection in my right lung. Corbet thinks I picked it up in St. Louis. I'm not contagious." I rubbed my cheek on his warm, naked chest.

"Are they running tests?"

I nodded. "Cindy told me that Corbet is setting up an appointment to see a specialist at John's Hopkins as soon as he can arrange it." I took a deep breath to calm my heart. I sniffled and wiped my nose again with my hand.

"The pills?"

"Antibiotics. Immune boosters. A whole cocktail. They're similar to the AIDS cocktail but a little different. I have to go pick up two more to add to the bunch this morning." I started shaking.

Max hugged me tighter. "You'll be okay." He kissed the top of my head.

I pushed off him and looked at my watch. I didn't have time to think about this. *Work. Take your mind off of the possibilities. Get to work. I've got work to do. I need to catch Carson.* "We need to get going." I wiped at the tears on my face and nose again.

Max brought my face to look at his. "Shouldn't you be resting?"

"What good would it do? I can't give into this." I looked away. I slowly picked myself up off the floor. "The doctor said as long as I feel up to it, I can maintain my normal routine. So I'm maintaining."

Max also stood and looked closely at me. "You haven't told anyone, have you?"

I shook my head. "I want to know what it is first. At first, I was afraid it was AIDS. I was worried that I had given it to you. I called and wanted to talk... You're the only one..." I looked away from him. "Then when it wasn't, and believe me we ran all the tests there are available, I sort of decided to wait." I could feel my muscles tightening up. If I didn't get moving, doing something, soon, I would start shaking.

Max rubbed my arms with his hands. "You're trembling."

I nodded and tried to move away from him. "Come on, Bauer. Let's go find us a kidnapper."

Max still held me by my arms, not letting go. "Are you sure this is how you want to do this? I think you need the support of family right now."

"They'd smother me, like when I was in the hospital. No. Please promise Max, that you won't tell anyone, including John."

Max's eyes delved deeply into mine. I felt as though he was reading my soul. Finally he nodded at me. "Okay." He leaned in and gave me a kiss on the lips, light and airy. "Can you grab me something for breakfast?" He hurried into the spare bedroom.

***

We sat silently in the woods near the old, abandoned farm house. John had left us a pair of binoculars. I had grabbed several water bottles and food to put in a cooler. Surveillance was long, boring and mind numbing. Before actually leaving town, we had stopped by the pharmacy and picked up my new pills. Max said nothing as I hopped back into the vehicle. Now it was about noon, and I was starting to get hungry, not something that happened often as of late.

"Ready for a sandwich?"

Max nodded, once more sweeping the clearing area. He accepted the sandwich, still with the binoculars plastered to his face. As he set them down on the ground, he looked at me. "I doubt the guy comes back."

"I know. John figures we'll do this for two or three days, then try something else." I opened the water bottle and faked a drink. I gagged and coughed as silently as I could for a second. Max looked alarmed and pounded me lightly on the back. "Are you okay?"

"Swallowed wrong." I managed to get out with a hesitant smile that I hoped looked confident. In reality, I'd been forcing myself not to cough all morning, but I could feel the heaviness in my lungs and knew it was going to come out sooner or later.

Max eyed me suspiciously, as though he didn't believe me but let it go. He suddenly glanced around behind us.

"What?"

"I need to take a leak."

"Use nature's bathroom."

Max stood up and quickly found a tree.

Silence once more settled around us.

I grabbed the binoculars and took a turn watching. Nothing. I was starting to really hate surveillance, again. We were sitting under a large tree in the shade, although the humidity was high. Since there was no breeze, it felt like we were sitting in a bowl of pudding, the air was so thick. And the gnats and other pesky bugs were out in small swarms. I would hate to be John or Rich and pull the evening slot. The mosquitoes had to be horrible at night. I swatted at a couple of pesky ones.

"Can I ask you a question?"

"Even if I say no, it's never stopped you before." I could almost hear his grin as I searched the old farm house again for movement.

"If I hadn't shown up at your dad's bar the other day, would you have tracked me down, especially when you found out about your problem?"

I set the binoculars in my lap and looked Max in the eyes. "I don't know. If it was something contagious, definitely. I wouldn't want to give it to…" I shrugged.

Max was just waiting, his expression hard to read.

"But it's not." I looked up at the tree. "Honestly, Max, I thought I screwed up. Abe has been pushing me to talk more about you. I hardly ever broach the subject and when he does, well, he says I strategically maneuver the conversation away from you." I looked at Max. "I guess I did and still do. Abe asked again yesterday about you. I'm not ready to think about us. I still have other issues."

"Like?"

"Craig's betrayal. Abe was working on that when I cancelled the sessions against his better judgment." I picked up a leaf and began stroking it. It was so fragile and broke in my hand. Then I began tearing at the leaf. When it was in little pieces, I picked up another and did the same.

Max watched me, then pulled up his knees and looked at the dirt. We were sitting on the ground on a blanket. It actually was quite comfortable.

"I… I found out from a 'source' earlier on the night that Craig and Robbie died, that Craig had had a liaison with an old girlfriend the night before our wedding. After I caught him with Wendy, I began to probe around. I became suspicious, with just-cause apparently. Craig, it seems, was only faithful for about two months after our marriage. I had been clueless. I loved him. I trusted him." Another leaf fell to pieces. "I gave him my heart, and the rat bastard not only broke it, he trampled it into the ground in a dance with his floozies." I tossed the next leaf away and picked up a stick. I could feel Max's stare but just stared at my hands as I began to break the stick into pieces.

"That night in the car, as we approached Highway 301, I confronted him about several of the times that he cheated on me. I was going to break the bastard, money-wise, and make him pay dearly. It was going to be a very messy divorce." I tossed the pieces of the stick away to pick up another. "When we stopped at the light, I remember glancing back at Robbie. He was sleeping peacefully. He was the only thing in my life not going into the crapper. The last thing Craig said to me, as he pulled out into traffic, was that he wanted to make the marriage work. He would change. He would get help. That he loved me." I picked up another stick and rubbed it between my fingers. Then I began to peel off the bark, until it was smooth. It took a few minutes.

I finally looked up. "When you said that you loved me, you threw me for a loop. I got scared. I ran. I admit it now. At the time… panic, I guess." I looked back down at the stick. It hurt to admit that I was wrong, although not as much as I originally thought when Abe proposed that I tell Max. I took a deep breath. "When I saw you in St. Louis, I about had a heart attack."

"Why?"

"The shock of seeing you." I groaned. "You looked gorgeous in a tux, especially the white tux jacket." I smiled, then looked back down at the stick. It suffered the same fate as the last one. "I almost wet myself. Then when Bart showed up, and I knew what you were thinking… Jerk. He knew too." I tossed the stick away in anger. "He figured out you liked me when you still lived here. Teased me about it afterward."

Max made a noise in his throat. Low and primal.

"Yeah. I almost had another heart attack at Dad's bar." I picked up a stick and dug in the dirt with it. "Then the hot tub. That was cruel."

"Yeah. Sorry. It was cruel. I guess I was being petty." He rocked slightly on his butt. "And talk about cleaning up. When I realized it was you standing in front of me in St. Louis… You were…" He made another noise in his throat instead of a word. "Anyway…" He shook his head.

"I didn't want to go to the charity ball. I hate that kind of function."

105

Max handed me a stick as all of the ones in front of me were gone.

I absentmindedly took it and began playing with it in my hands. I was moving it from finger to finger using just the fingers on one hand. "The whole sick thing is that Jimmy touched a soft spot in my heart that I thought had healed. Kids, gotta love'em." I sighed. "And Carmine." I looked back at the house. Dropping the stick, I picked up the binoculars and did another sweep of the place. Nothing.

"Where do we stand in all this?"

I swallowed and slowly lowered the binoculars. "I don't know, Max. I like you. You make me feel…" I didn't know how to explain my feelings. "…warm again." I picked up the stick again. "I just don't know if… I can't…" Max was just watching me; I could see him out of the corner of my eye. "When you go this time, could you at least leave me your phone number and maybe return my calls?" My eyes flooded with tears. I tried swallowing them back. "I won't bother you often. And I can't hope that you'll wait around for me to stop being a nutcase, but maybe we could still be friends. I don't actually have too many." I looked up.

Max reached out, pulled my face up, and kissed me. "Who said I was leaving?"

"You will. I'll drive you away."

"You drive me insane, yes." Max kept my face pointed at his. "I'll say it again… I love you, Mel. And I'm sorry Craig hurt you so deeply, but not all men are rat bastards."

I managed a slight grin for him.

"Give me a hug, you crazy woman." He pulled me into a tight hug. I went to move, but he shook his head. "Relax." He moved slightly and still holding me, leaned against the tree. "Just relax. I want to hold you for awhile."

I sighed and snuggled into his arms, even though it was hot. It felt so good, that for once, I didn't think about being sick or anything but his arms comforting me. It wasn't long and I was out like a light.

***

106

I felt someone stroking my hair. I snuggled into the hand without waking up. It was a gentle stroke, tender. The fingers ran over my cheeks, barely touching my skin. It felt like someone was running a current down the length of my body. I moved, still half asleep and oh so comfortable, except I was hot. I murmured unintelligent words, even to my ears.

"Shhh." A soft, quiet voice whispered back.

I wiggled further into the comfort and sighed. It felt like I was warm and snuggly in a quilt in the dead of winter, when you're just waking and not wanting to get out of bed.

A light kiss touched my forehead.

I jerked awake and opened my eyes to see Max's blue eyes staring into mine. I was momentarily frozen. *Where? Where was I?* I twisted to move but was held in his arms.

"Relax."

It hit me like a tornado. "The farm." I pushed his arms away and sat up. The shadows had lengthened. I quickly looked at my watch. I had been asleep for four hours. "How weak of me." Anger at myself burst inside. "How could I have…"

Max interrupted me with a kiss on the lips. "Nothing happened. I sat and watched." He smiled. "Except for a deer working its way though the woods, there was no movement at all."

I jumped up in anger and paced a few steps away then turned. As I turned, I felt the bubbling, choking feeling in my chest. My right hand automatically moved to the side of my chest.

Max jumped up. "Mel? What's wrong?"

I tried desperately to quell the cough making its way up my bronchioles. I couldn't breathe. Then it came out. I hacked and coughed. Finally I felt the lump of phlegm. With a turn of my head, I spit it out, then just stood bent over trying to catch my breath.

Max's hands were holding my sides as I bent over. I gasped for air. He pulled me up and held me against his chest in a gentle embrace. His hands were massaging my back muscles, his head laid on mine. "Easy. Slow your breathing or you'll hyperventilate. Deep breaths, Tiger."

I nodded and closed my eyes. Now my lung and chest hurt, again. The deep breaths actually hurt. I took shallower gulps of air and felt much better. I pushed off of Max's chest and wiped the tears from coughing. "Sorry."

Max put his arm around me. "Let's gather the stuff and leave."

"No."

"He's not coming back, at least for awhile. I was going to suggest leaving sooner, but you collapsed on me, and I didn't want to wake you." Max smiled. "He's not dumb enough to come back right away."

I thought about it. Rich, John and I all knew that too. I think we were grabbing at straws to find the girl. I nodded and pulled my cell phone out of my pocket. "Hey, Rich."

"What's up? Did Carson show?"

"No, Max and I are pulling the plug. He's not showing."

Rich sighed. "Yeah, John and I have been talking about it, and we came to the same conclusion. I was getting ready to call you. Listen, before you head into town, drive past the old farm house with the renter. Peek and see if the truck is there. If it is, call, don't do anything. We'll get the state police there lickety-split."

"Got it."

Rich hesitated. "Hey, are you okay?"

"Yeah. Why?"

There was a pause on the line. I could almost see Rich deciding if it would be worth the trouble to broach a subject. "You haven't looked right lately."

"I'm just tired."

Another hesitation. "Okay. John wants to talk to Max. He's out talking to people. He said to have Max call after seven."

"What about?"

"I don't know. John didn't say."

"Okay."

Another pause. "Take it easy, sis."

"Always." I hung up the phone. Max was finishing folding the blanket and arranging things on the cooler. "John wants you to call him at your convenience tonight after seven."

Max glanced up at me quickly, his eyes betraying that he knew what it was about. "Okay. Ready?"

I went to grab the one side of the cooler but Max shook his head.

"I got it." Everything was on top of the cooler.

Anger flared. "Bauer, I am not helpless, and stop this right now. I won't have it."

Max looked at the cooler, then back at me.

I was breathing faster, and I knew my hands were clenched.

With a deliberate move, he picked the blanket and binoculars off the cooler and tossed them to me. "Here help me carry this." With an air, as though I had not spoken, he picked up the remaining items and moved through the woods toward where we had hidden the Jeep.

I huffed once. My right lung was still aching from the coughing, but I refused to give into the feelings and just trudged along behind him. Finally we got to the Jeep.

Since he was slightly ahead of me, he had already tossed the cooler into the back, and then as I reached the vehicle, he grabbed stuff out of my hands. "You're getting slow." He looked at me with teasing eyes.

I just rubbed my chest.

"Does it hurt?"

"Yeah." I dug into my pockets and took out the keys. "Thanks for holding me."

The area around Max's eyes relaxed, and he reached out for me. "I'll hold you anytime, Tiger. Anytime."

I once more leaned into his embrace. "I'm scared, Max." The words just tumbled out. It was then that I realized that I had never admitted it, even to myself.

"I know." He hugged me tight. "Me too." Max kissed the top of my head. "Me too."

We stood there for a couple more seconds, then as if by some unspoken word, we both let go at the same time. I moved to the driver's side and he hopped into the passenger side.

The drive past the farm house showed that no one was home. We drove into the nearest town and stopped at the convenience store for cold drinks. The ones in the cooler were not cold anymore. I opened my apple juice and leaned on the Jeep.

Max was using the bathroom, again.

That poor girl. She has to be terrified. I closed my eyes to think. *Now that we had spooked him, where would he go? This is a bad thing we've done. He's on the run now and desperate. A dangerous situation for Carmine.*

"He's gone," I said softly.

"Who's gone?"

I jumped. I hadn't realized that Max was standing in front of me. "We spooked him. I wouldn't be surprised if he isn't long gone." I looked around the area.

"Maybe. Maybe not."

I twisted my head to look at him. "What do you mean?"

Max shifted on his feet. "We had a case in California, Ox and me. We were trying to catch a pedophile. He had already killed three boys. We almost caught him but he got away. Like you, I was sure he was long gone. Ox assured me that he knew the area, and he would probably stay put, otherwise he'd have to check out a whole new area. You know, find a new place to pick up boys. We waited and through sheer, hard work, with a little luck thrown in, we finally got him."

I studied Max closely. He was rubbing his keys in his pocket. His fingers were turning the keys over and over. "It must have been satisfying to put him in cuffs."

Max's eyes flicked to the side of the road as a car whooshed past us. He turned to watch it before answering. "I shot him. Killed him." His voice was flat and there was no emotion at all. Max turned back to me. "We still have a chance with this guy. The file you showed me seems to make it out that Carson liked Trenton and this place. With his past history, I'd have to say he'll stick here."

"A hunch?"

Max's shoulders lifted. "Call it what you will."

"Ox?"

Max's gaze swept the roadway again before landing back on me. "My partner in Wharfer's Point."

"The one that died?"

Max nodded, his feet shifting again in the dirt. His hands were still in his pockets working the keys.

I studied him. He didn't want to talk about it. "So, Mister Former Policeman, how do we find Brady Carson?"

Max smiled. I could see he was relieved at my letting the subject drop. "I was thinking, did he stay anywhere else in this area? And you had a footnote in the file that said he hunted while in Illinois. Where? Anywhere besides the farm?"

I just looked at him. They were really good suggestions. "Let's find out."

Chapter 9

I sat in the Lazyboy at home trying to sleep. Max and I had worked long into the night trying to find more information about Carson but hadn't turned up much of anything. It was frustrating. After we got home, I was dead tired, and Max sent me to bed right away. I remember him joining me later, but he merely shh'ed me to sleep, placing an arm over me, and I drifted off. Later, I woke needing to cough up more phlegm. I struggled to keep it down, but I knew the body wanted it out.

Max was laying on his back, mouth slightly open. A very light snoring was coming from him. I quickly slid out of bed and moved into the laundry room at the far end of the house and hacked until it came out. When I returned to the bedroom, Max had rolled over and placed an arm under his head. He looked like a little boy, except for the beard and mustache.

I knew from experience that I would continue to cough if I laid back down. It was better to just get up and move around, so I moved into the living room with a pillow and light blanket.

Now I sat there thinking. The upright position allowed me to sleep without the wheezing I knew I had to be making while I slept. Closing my eyes, I found my mind drifting back to California and the time I spent with Max. They were good memories.

A noise startled me. I opened my eyes to find Max standing in the doorway watching me.

"Can't sleep?"

"I woke up to cough. I didn't want to wake you. This position is better for the lung. Lets me rest better."

Max nodded and headed to the kitchen. "Do you want a drink?"

"I got water, thanks." I took another drink and set it back on the floor.

He returned with a glass of water. After scratching his chest, he settled himself on the couch, his head facing me. Pulling the couch blanket over him he smiled. "You have a comfortable couch."

"Thanks."

We heard a muted ringing of a phone. It was Max's cell. He hurried to get it and answered as he moved back into the living room. "Yeah?... Oh, for God's sake Tiffany! Do you know what time it is?" He twisted around on the couch to see the clock on the wall. "Yes, I was asleep... Yeah, yeah. Okay. What do you want?" Max rubbed his face. "I'm not flying to Rio... No!... Good, then go party for another twenty four hours... I told you twice, I am not marrying you. Go propose to Adrian or whatever his name is... Good, you do that... Yeah, send a wedding invitation to the business address... I'm sure I will. Goodbye." Max hung up the phone and blew out his breath.

"Women problems?"

Max's head snapped up. "My only woman problem is you, Mel." He smiled. "They're just annoyances."

"A marriage proposal is an annoyance?"

"God, you don't understand. These people, how they operate." He waved his hand in the air. "When I started traveling with Grandma, it became known that I was single. I have been hit upon by every single, and every not so single woman. In the past four months, I've averaged about one proposal a week. Tiffany is the latest."

"Sophia?"

"Before Tiffany. Sophia lives in Italy."

"Did you sleep with them?"

Max stared at me in the near darkness of the room. "Do you really want to know?"

I swallowed. My emotions flared raw. Feelings of betrayal popped into my head and my heart sank. *Was it Craig all over again? No, he wasn't Craig, and we really had no relationship at all. Why am I being this way?* I saw blue eyes in the darkness watching me. "Yeah. I do."

"I slept with Sophia once. None of the others." Max kept studying me. "I was drunk when she took me to bed. In the morning afterward, she kept asking me who Mel was."

I swallowed again. He had made love to her but was thinking of me.

"She looks sort of like you. Taller and heavier, but the same hair and eyes. I made love that night to her body. Earlier in the evening, I heard a lady laughing in the square where the party was going on. I swear it was your laugh. I followed it, and of course it wasn't you. I started drinking heavily. Sophia was the granddaughter of a friend of Grandma's. I left Sophia that morning in tears because I wouldn't make love to her again."

The silence drug out. It was dead quiet in the room. Max's voice broke the stillness. "I want to be honest with you, Mel. I never intended on sleeping with anyone. It just happened. I was weak and drunk. I'm sorry."

I blushed although it was dark and he maybe couldn't see it. He felt like he had betrayed me. Us. "You have nothing to be sorry about."

Max's head lifted. "I don't ever want to hurt you. I want you to know that you can trust me, in all things."

"I know that. And I'm not really hurt by your actions. A little jealous maybe." I smiled. "Trust has always been a touchy subject with me."

"And Craig ruined it for all of us."

"No. Well, yes. I guess. I'm trying to trust again."

Max slid off the couch and knelt on the floor next to the Lazy Boy. His face was even with mine. "You can trust me, Mel."

I leaned over and kissed him. "I'll try. I can't promise…"

Max kissed me with an aggressiveness that took me back. Then he tempered it with a gentle nip to the lower lip. He pulled back and looked me in the eye. "How do you feel?"

"To be honest Max… Horny, but I'm also very tired."

"Me too." His eyes got a down right sexy look. He kissed me again. This time it was a long drawn out, shake the world until it ends and take your breath way, forever type kiss. His fingertips lightly caressed my arms and neck. The shock waves ran up and down my body. He had done something similar in California, and it had been awesome. It

114

seemed like hours before we broke the kiss. And even though I was tired, I wanted more.

Max chuckled as he watched me. "But you need to rest. Another time, Tiger." He grabbed the blanket, that had somehow made it to the floor, and covered me up. Tucking in the sides, he gave me light kisses. When he finished, he slid onto the couch and covered himself up. "Sleep. I'm not going anywhere."

I sighed and he chuckled again.

"I love you, Mel. Go to sleep." Then he closed his eyes and snuggled into the couch.

I watched him for a few minutes, a smile playing at my lips.

"You need to rest. Stop staring at me."

Now I chuckled and closed my eyes. Content.

***

I sat with my head in both my hands reading paperwork from the last two medications I had picked up. I hadn't had the chance yesterday, and I wanted to know what the side effects were. I sighed. I hoped none of this stuff happened. I would be worse than the coughing, tired, achy feeling that I had.

Max moved into the room in almost silence.

I looked up to see him smile. I nodded back then went back to reading. I flipped over the last page and finished it as Max rummaged in my fridge.

"Hungry? Can I fix you something?"

"I can't eat for another forty minutes, but thanks." I glanced at the clock. "I'll force something down then."

Max had paused at the open fridge door and looked at me. "Why?"

"Why wait on the food?"

Max nodded.

"I can't take one of the pills with food. The other four need food. One at lunch time. These…" I motioned to the two new bottles, "…are three times a day with food, but not with the purple pill. So I'll have to take them an hour after I take the purple one with breakfast." I shook my head. "I hate this. I'm chained to these stupid pills."

Max sat opposite me and took my hand. "It's just until you find out what's causing this."

"Hopefully." I gave him a tiny smile. "Thanks for last night, even though I wanted more. You were wonderful."

Max grinned.

"Where did you learn to do that?"

"It's a strange story."

I motioned with my hand to the pill bottles. "I have forty minutes."

"Okay…" Max nodded and stood up to retrieve a glass of juice. He offered to get me one, but I touched the bottle and shook my head. He reseated himself with a full glass. "I was travelling one summer with my parents in France. We stopped at a small village a couple hours outside of Paris for some reason. I really don't remember. I was pissed at my parents because I had wanted to spend the summer with friends in England. Anyway…" He took a big drink. "I hiked away from the group and found myself lost in a woods. I came out in a clearing to find an old sheep herder's cottage or shed or something."

"How old were you?"

"Fifteen." He took another drink. "Anyway, out walked this lovely lady. She was a goddess."

I watched as Max's eyes became opaque. I could tell he was lost in the memory. I smiled watching him.

"Following her was a man. Both were naked." His eyes turned to mine and he smiled. "Yeah. I was fifteen. You can guess what sort of a reaction I had."

I chuckled.

Max continued to smile. "They headed to a small meadow area that was near me. I stayed hidden. I watched them make love. It was the most incredible thing I ever saw. I was so fascinated. And I saw him doing something similar to what I did last night." Another drink. "When they finished, they both started laughing. They knew I was there apparently. The man got dressed then motioned for me."

I gave him a disbelieving look.

"I swear…" He held his hand up as if to testify. "He asked if I enjoyed watching his wife and him make love. I blushed bright red I'm sure. I admitted I did and told him I was lost and could he point out the way back to the village. He said he was headed that way and would give me a ride. While we drove, I apologized again to him."

"How old were they?"

Max shrugged. "I would guess in their thirties, a lot older than me. Anyway, the man laughed and said it was okay that I watched. No harm done. I probably blushed again, I was so embarrassed. As we reached the village, the man turned to me and said something I never forgot. He said, 'If you want to make love to a woman, think of her needs first. A woman needs to be stroked and appreciated.'" Max drained his glass. "After I thanked him and got out of his car, he made a motion for me to return. 'Dedicate your life to love, son. A woman's skin is her most sensitive organ, remember that.' Then he drove away. His words have played in my mind ever since." Max smiled at the fact that I was staring at him.

"Is that a true story?"

"Reality is far stranger than fiction." Max moved the glass between his hands on the table. "What's the game plan for today?"

"For me, in to the office to see if anything broke. Tomorrow, I have pre-employment verification checks for our business clients. Takes all morning, but it makes Fridays go faster. Saturday, I'm stuck babysitting most of the evening for Ralph." I stood up and placed the new pill bottles in the basket on the counter. "I'm going to take a shower." I stretched, moving my shoulder around a bit. It really ached this morning.

"Does it hurt?" Max asked leaning back in his chair.

"Different joints ache on different days, that's the thing that has Corbet troubled. The shoulder really hurts today." I headed away from the room.

"Mel, what do you want for breakfast? I'll have it ready when you get out."

I glanced back. "Just toast. I usually have to force it down. My appetite is gone."

Max frowned. "I noticed in St. Louis that you've lost weight. You look really good now, but I think you need to make yourself eat more. You'll start to look sick if you loose much more weight."

I nodded. I knew that. I headed to the master shower and when I finished, Max had a meal on the table. He had cooked eggs and toast and orange juice waiting. I sighed.

"Just try eating." He sat with me, and we ate in silence.

I forced a small portion down. I felt slightly nauseous. I shook my head at his offer for more.

"You did pretty good." Max frowned. "What?"

"I hate this." I stood up taking my plate to the sink. "I don't like to be babied and coddled."

Max joined me at the counter. He took me into his arms from behind. "I'm not babying you. You get to clean up my mess. I just wanted you to eat something more than toast." He kissed the back of my neck. "I'm going to…"

The phone rang, and I picked it up without moving out of his arms. "Hello?" I merely listened then thanked them.

"What?" Max asked as he softly kissed my neck again.

"That was Corbet's office. The first appointment that is available with Dr. Changri at John's Hopkins is three weeks." I sighed. "I don't know if I can do all these pills for that long."

Max didn't speak but turned me around. "Just take it one day at a time." He smiled then glanced at his watch and grabbed his cell out of his pocket. He dialed a number as he kissed me. "Harvey, it's Max Bauer. I have a question for you…" He gave me another light kiss then headed away from the kitchen to take a shower.

About twenty minutes later Max walked back into the kitchen to find me talking on the phone. I was still trying to track down another of Bart's relatives and so far was having no luck. I checked in with the guys at the office, but they didn't care that I wasn't in yet. It was nearing ten.

I held up my hand so Max would wait as I began speaking. "Okay, well, could you have him call me as soon as possible…"

"Can I just give him a message? It would be easier."

"No. It's a touchy subject, and I'd rather talk to him first."

"I guess try later in the evening around eight, maybe he might be here."

My thanks was only heard by the dial tone.

Max slid onto the chair next to mine. When I finished, he asked, "What are you doing tonight and more importantly all day tomorrow?"

I bunched up my face. "I already told you. Work. Why?"

Max shook his head. "Go pack. You also need to call Corbet's office and have them fax your records to Changri's office today."

"What?"

"You have an appointment with him at eleven tomorrow morning." Max smiled.

My mouth dropped open.

"We have a flight out of St. Louis at four today for Baltimore. I'll drive. I need to return the BMW to St. Louis anyway." He glanced at his watch.

"But—"

"I've even thought of an excuse for Rich and John..." Bauer paused. "We can visit Mr. Hernandez in Pennsylvania. I'm sure he'll see us after I explain who I am."

"How did—"

Max leaned over and kissed me. "I've never used Grandma's money and influence before. I called Harvey Kartel in New York. He's in charge of one of the funds on the East Coast. We give regularly to John's Hopkins. When I explained the problem to Harvey, he said the three week appointment was just wrong. When I got out of the shower, he called back and said that he had gotten a sooner appointment."

I made a face.

"Money talks. It's not fair, but that's the way the world works. I've seen it demonstrated lots of times. Let me do this for you. Please. I want you well."

I looked down at the pill information sheets still sitting on the table. I didn't want to take these pills for three weeks. One of them was already making me nauseous. It could only get worse. I raised my eyes. "Okay."

Max's smile lit up his face. "That was easier than I thought it was going to be."

I smirked. "I'll call Jason and see if we can use his guest house."

"No need," Max said standing up to get a drink. "I've already arranged to have Grandma's Annapolis house waiting for us. Grandma used to live in Annapolis. It's a really nice house." He looked at me as he closed the fridge.

I was trying to sort through my feelings at this sudden turn of events. I felt both smothered and comforted at the same time.

Max's eyes changed. "So, you get to buy our meals on this trip. Deal?"

The feeling moved to a warm glow. "I guess. If I must."

"What are you waiting for? Call the doctor's office and get packed."

***

We stopped at the office on our way out of town. John and Rich were both in, which was a change. Max explained to them that his grandmother needed him in Annapolis for two days and he was taking me with him. In exchange, we would track down Hernandez and ask him about Ava Papios. With a glance between them, they agreed.

The trip to St. Louis was uneventful. I even fell asleep part of the time. An employee of one of his grandmother's businesses was waiting for us at the airport to take care of the BMW. With just minutes to spare, we grabbed our tickets and headed to the concourse. Shortly thereafter we boarded the plane. I was surprised when we were seated in first class. I had never flown first class before, and Max found that amusing.

We landed at BWI in Baltimore and found another car, this time a Lexus, waiting for us. A passing of the keys from the man to Max, with a 'Have a good day Mr. Bauer,' and we were off to his grandmother's house.

Annapolis traffic hadn't changed from what I remembered. As we headed toward the Chesapeake Bay, I wondered what sort of house his grandmother would own. I soon recognized the area of Annapolis we were in, and if I wasn't mistaken, she lived near the Bay itself. We cleared a small hill and there was only one house in front of us.

And what a house it was. It was a large mansion that faced onto a small cove right off of the Chesapeake Bay, which I later learned had ten bedrooms. It was gorgeous. I looked around in awe to be honest. It was huge! The house was two stories of white magnificence. The lawns were manicured to perfection. I could smell the Bay and knew that this was one of those houses that Craig had lusted after. I was sure she had and large shoreline with boat dock behind the house.

"Wow."

"Yeah. Grandpa bought it when it was a run down dump a long time ago. That was obviously before development hit the Bay. He bought out the two neighboring properties because he liked privacy." Max pointed with one hand. "There's a swimming pool, with hot tub attached, in the back yard behind the garage over there. And Grandpa's pride and joy, his sailboat, might be docked at the water. It depends on who is staying here."

"Jeez."

Max chuckled again as the front door opened and a middle-aged lady stood at the door. We moved in that direction. "Hi Mrs. Majors. Mel, this is Mrs. Majors, the keeper of the Annapolis estate. Mrs. Majors, Melissa Addison."

"Maxie, my boy. I haven't seen you in awhile. Mrs. Grasicolli said that you were traveling with her. Come and give me a hug." She held out her arms and the two of them hugged. She swiped at his beard. "Normally I don't like facial hair, but on you it looks good. Not like your father." She turned to me. "So this is Mel."

I glanced at Max who blushed. "I think Grandma likes to gossip."

Both of them laughed, so I chuckled with them. "Nice to meet you." I held out my hand, but she pulled me into a hug.

"Any *friend* of Max's is welcome here. Come in." She gestured to the house.

"Do you live here?" I asked walking in and trying to keep the wonder out of my voice as I got my first impression of the entryway. It was a full two stories high with a grand sweeping staircase like you see in movies. It reminded me of *Gone With the Wind*.

"Oh God no." Mrs. Majors chuckled. "I live out back, over the garage. One apartment is mine. One is Clarence's, the chauffeur. This place is a museum."

Max laughed, then looked at my puzzled look. "Inside family joke. Thanks for being able to put us up at the last minute. I hope it wasn't a bother."

She gave his cheek a light pat. "For you, never. I did have to put you in the small room. *Phillip* is in the suite for the next several weeks." The way she said 'Phillip' made me think she didn't like him. "Make yourself at home Mel. If either of you needs anything, you know how to reach me." She gave Max a peck on the cheek. She disappeared down the hall to the right.

Max started to head to the left.

I stood looking around.

Max walked over and gave me a kiss. Lips only. "Come on. I'll show you around in a bit." He glanced at his watch. "If we want to make it to Pennsylvania tonight we need to be heading out soon." He started to walk away again.

Slowly I followed, looking around, taking in all of the opulence. I only saw things like this on TV. "Seriously. You lived here?"

Max chuckled. "Yeah. My room was on the other side of the house. I'll show you later. Mrs. Majors put us up in the small bedroom." He lead the way past several doors.

"She's nice."

"Yeah. Most of the rest of the family treat her like a maid. Except Grandma. They act like old friends. I always treated Mrs. Majors like an aunt." He smiled. "She saved my butt more times than I care to admit." When I opened my mouth, he shook his head. "Those are stories for another time. Here we are." He swung open the door.

This room was a living room about the size of my apartment over the Silver Moon. The whole apartment.

"The bedroom is through that door." Max pointed, setting his suitcase on the nearest chair. "Bathroom." He pointed at another door. "And a small kitchenette with fridge and microwave." There was a small hallway that curved.

"And this is the *small* bedroom? This is almost bigger than my house."

"To my cousins, this is tiny. I actually like this room better than the big suite. Actually so does Grandma. Her room isn't much bigger."

I shook my head and headed to the bedroom. When I opened the door, I gasped. The window and French doors opened to a small deck that faced the Bay.

"What?" Max joined me.

"The view!"

Max chuckled again. "The suite has a better view, but the best view is from the edge of the swimming pool." He pointed to the right to the pool.

"I bet." I turned, and as I dropped my bag on the bed, I raised my eyebrows. "With no neighbors, skinny dipping must be fun."

He laughed, grabbed me and kissed me like in my living room. I was moving him toward the bed when he stopped us. "Don't distract me. We have a job to do. Pennsylvania." He grabbed my hand and led me out of the room. As we exited the front of the house, we saw a large white limo pulling into the circular drive.

"Crap," Max said softly under his breath.

I looked at him puzzled.

"It's my cousin, Phillip. He's a jerk. I was hoping to avoid running into him." Max put on a fake smile and greeted his cousin as the man stepped out of the car. "Hello, Phillip."

"Max," Phillip said in that snooty, upper crust way. "Who do we have here?" he asked looking at me.

"This is Mel Addison," Max said, introducing us. "Mel, Phillip Grasicolli."

Phillip's eyes took in my less than casual dress. Max and I were both in jeans and comfortable shirts, mine was a polo. Phillip, on the other hand, wore a three piece suit, that I swear was straight from Italy. Even his shoes screamed money.

"Pleasure," Phillip said, then seemed to dismiss me. "Is Grandmother here? Are you staying at the house?"

"Just us. Grandma's in Texas. Don't worry Phillip, Mel and I are staying in the small bedroom. Mrs. Majors already informed me that you have the suite."

"Oh!" Phillip's eyes flicked to me. "You normally don't bring your dates home."

Max flinched, but the smile stayed in place.

I smiled at Phillip and walked closer to him. I hated snooty people. "I'm not his date. I'm only sleeping with him." I made smoochy sounds at Phillip, touched his chin and walked away.

123

Max snorted a chuckle.

I heard a slight intake of breath from Phillip; as I turned I swayed my hips a bit. "Come on, Maxie-baby, we got things to do."

Phillip was now staring at me with mouth open.

Max paused next to him. "Close your mouth Phillip. You don't want to spoil your image." He smiled a bigger smile at his cousin and walked away. Max started laughing at me as I was still sauntering my way to the Lexus.

I turned to get in the car and gave a little finger wave at Phillip, who was now staring with mouth closed. I glanced at Max who was getting in the car still laughing.

Max turned to me and leaned over for a kiss. He shook his head and drove off. "You make my day, Mel."

"I hate snooty people."

Max nodded. "Phillip is one of the snootiest." He licked his lips. "*That* was sexy. I love your tight jeans."

"Pennsylvania my dear man."

***

I shifted my weight on my feet as Max was talking to Mr. Hernandez on his porch. He didn't appear happy to see us. Yes, he had received Max's phone calls. Hernandez still hadn't opened the screen door. Max was trying to convince him to talk to us.

"...My Dad felt that you might be able to help us."

Hernandez glanced at me and back to Max. "Maximillian was a great boss." He paused considering. "Again, why do you need to speak with Ms. Papios?"

"She worked as a nanny for a lady a long time ago. The son is trying to find out who his real parents are. He is trying to find out the truth about his birth. He hired the private investigative firm that we work for to find out, if we can, who his real parents are and where he was born. Ava Papios might be able to help us. She doesn't have to speak with anyone in the family."

Hernandez seemed to be considering.

"Mr. Hernandez…" I interjected. "We won't even tell the client where we found you or her. She can remain an anonymous source. We've done that before."

He still seemed undecided. Finally, he sighed. "You wait here. I will call her and find out if she wants to talk to you. Is that acceptable?"

"Absolutely," Max said.

Hernandez closed the front door on us.

Max stepped off the porch and shrugged.

"A private investigator firm that 'we' work for?"

"I can lie with the best them." He gave me a kiss on the lips.

"Purely minor league," I said and sat down on the step. I was tired again. My hands ached this time. I clenched and unclenched them to ease the ache.

Max sat too and watched but said nothing.

The door opened after about five minutes. Hernandez looked out at us. "Come on in."

Max and I stood up, both surprised. We followed Hernandez into the house and through the living room. He wound his way to the back of the house and out into a sun room. The side windows were open and the breeze made it a very pleasant setting.

Seated in a wheel chair by a table was a woman who was remarkably close to the computer generated composite Bart had made. It was uncanny. Max motioned for me to take the lead.

I walked over the table and motioned to sit.

"Please." Her voice was very soft and melodic.

"Ms. Papios…"

"Mrs. Hernandez, actually."

I smiled. "We won't take up much of your time…" I quickly relayed the entire Bart thing for her. Her expression never changed, but she did keep glancing between Max and me. "So, you can see how Mr. Hessor is confused about his parents' identity. Since you were his nanny in his early years, he wants to know if you know anything at all that might help us."

"He remembered me?"

I nodded. "He only recalled your first name, although he remembered it as Anna."

Ava laughed a soft thrilling sound. "He used to call me that, I remember. He had trouble with the 'v.'" She continued to smile as though lost in memory. Her eyes refocused on me. "Is Madeline still living?"

"Yes, although she is currently doing time in prison."

"She finally got caught." It was a statement not a question.

I chuckled. "Ironically, by my dad."

Another trilled laugh. "Serves her right. She was such a nasty person. She never treated her hired help more than a shade above slaves. I worked five horrible years for her."

"So you weren't there when Bart was born?"

Ava shook her head. "I started caring for little Bart when he was one. He was already a terror by then." She smiled again at a memory.

"Do you have any clue as to who his parents are?"

Another shake of her head. "I took over for another nanny. She was an elderly lady then, maybe around fifty. I doubt she is still alive."

I looked down at my hands. Another dead end. This was hopeless.

"Have you tried speaking with Madeline herself? I'm sure she knows who Bart's real parents are."

"Bart says he has spoken with her many times. Our firm has not spoken with her, nor will we." I gave her a smile. "My oldest brother, who is part owner of the firm, was a police officer. And the other partner is diametrically opposed to drugs. So you see, none of us would want to speak with her."

Ava thought about the situation.

"I have one more question, Mrs. Hernandez."

She looked at me.

"This is merely for my information. I've been curious about why you disappeared after you left Griffin Industries. It seemed odd. I won't relay that to anyone if you answer; it's merely personal curiosity."

Ava looked deeply into my eyes. She seemed to come to an understanding with herself or something. She slightly nodded. "Madeline Hessor threatened me when I was working at Griffin. That was a couple of years after I stopped working for her. There was a big shake up with her drug people, I found out later. She thought I had been approached to help kidnap Bart. No matter how hard I tried to convince her that I could never harm Bart, she refused to believe me. She threatened my life if Bart was ever kidnapped. Bart was maybe ten at the time." Ava sighed. "I spoke with Herman. We were lovers. He asked me to marry him and move with him the next week to a different branch office. I got a fake ID and we were married."

Now it all made sense. "Well, thank you for your help anyway." I shook her hand and stood up. "Thanks for talking with us."

"Certainly," Ava said softly.

We were almost to the door of the sunroom when she called my name. I turned, glancing at Max with a puzzled look. "Yes?"

"Tanto. Martinez Tanto worked as a maintenance man before I got there. He was always in the know about things. He might be able to help you." She paused then looked at her hand. "He is my cousin and got me the job with the Hessors. He lives close by. I will call him and see if he will talk to you."

I nodded in thanks.

Thirty minutes later we were seated in another house on a couch. A much older man sat with oxygen on. His raspy voice was sometimes hard to understand. His emphysema was bad today, he informed us as we sat down.

"So you want to know about little Bart?" His Mexican accent was still heavy.

I went through the whole story again for him. Martin nodded as I spoke.

"Bart was brought to the house when he was around six months, if I remember right. Nellie, his old nurse made such a fuss over him. He was a cutie. Ava took over when Nellie couldn't take care of him any longer."

"Do you by any chance know who his parents are? Did you hear any rumors back then?"

Martin coughed and hacked up some spittle. He wiped it on a cloth. "Sorry. I don't know. The whole family was gone for almost a full year from the house. It was the easiest year I spent working for the Hessors. Madeline and her husband were so demanding. Very picky people. Mr. Hessor and a young couple arrived first. Then Madeline shortly after. I can't remember how long, maybe a couple of weeks or less. About two months later or so the baby and Nellie showed up. We were not introduced to the couple."

"This couple… Can you describe them?"

He motioned to his wife. "I don't much remember them now. But I think I might have a picture…" He turned to his wife and spoke quickly in Spanish. She answered back, then disappeared from the room. "If Maria can find the picture, you may take it. I would like it returned when you are finished though. It is the only picture I have of my first wife. She died about two years after this picture was taken. We were celebrating an anniversary. If I am not mistaken, the young couple are in the background of the picture."

It took a while, apparently, to find the picture, but finally his wife returned with the photo. She handed it to Martin who looked at it closely. He held it out to me. "It is not a very clear picture of them."

I took it and looked closely. Sure enough, it was grainy and starting to fade. The young couple was seated in the background at a bench, amusingly watching the party in front of them. I could see Mr. Tanto and a lovely young woman with him. Several other people were around and all of Mexican heritage. I held it out to Max.

"Thank you, Mr. Tanto. I'll make a copy of it and have it mailed back to you as soon as possible. I appreciate you speaking with me and helping us out."

"Your last name is Addison. Did I hear correctly?"

I nodded.

"A police officer named Addison came to the house after Madeline was arrested. He interviewed us. He was very nice. He didn't exhibit the usual prejudice."

I smiled. "That was my Dad."

Tanto seemed to be thinking. "I believe his name was Richard Addison. Correct?"

I nodded, the smile getting bigger. "You have a great memory. Did he interview all of the help?"

"I believe so."

I turned to Max. "Why didn't we think of that? Dad would know more of the help. Right under our nose."

Max chuckled as he handed the photo back. "If he is anything like the old cops I trained under, he probably still has his notes on the case."

Tanto smiled. "Officer Addison even helped us out. We were out of a job since her property was seized. He helped get us new work, which led to me working for a firm in Cleveland, Ohio. It was there that I got training and eventually became a manager of the plant. I have always wanted to thank the officer but never tried to find him. Could you relay my thanks?"

"Absolutely." I shook Mr. Tanto's hand.

***

The drive back to Annapolis was pleasant. The sun was setting and it was a nice evening. The case was advancing slowly. I looked at the picture again.

"I could digitize a copy and send it to John tonight when we get to Grandma's house," Max said watching me concentrate on the picture.

"Yeah. I just wish I could have reached Rich or John. They could go talk to Dad. And he thinks his notes are still in the basement." I set the photo down on my lap. Closing my eyes, I relaxed.

"Are you tired?"

"Yeah."

"Hungry? We never ate supper."

"We can stop if you want. I'm not hungry. Actually I feel nauseous. I guess I should have taken that last pill with food." I opened my eyes and looked at Max.

He smiled. "I can wait until we get to the house."

"So…" I smiled back. "If you travel all the time, where do you call home now?"

Max shook his head. "I don't really have one single home. I don't think I ever did. At least not until I was older and refused to play their games."

"Games?"

"My family expects certain… things. I, at the time, didn't want to be just another cog in the Grasicolli empire. I wanted to do something with my life." Max shrugged. "I enjoyed being a police office."

"Why did you quit?" I laid my head back on the seat and watched him.

He didn't answer right away, but I could see emotions working on his face. "When you left, I felt empty. I started drinking, again. At that point, I realized I was more of a threat to the squad than the criminals. I quit the force because I didn't care anymore."

I grimaced. I hadn't realized that I had hurt him this deeply.

Max glanced at me. "Grandpa died a month after you left. He was sickly anyway. At the reading of his will, which I didn't attend, he left me the bulk of his personal estate, including the shipping company."

"Why?"

"Grandpa made his money with his hands. He was the only one to really support me in my quest to live a life apart from the family. Even Grandma wanted me to toe the line. He left me a letter with the lawyer. He told me that he thought I was the only one who would appreciate the company, as I was the only one who knew what a hard day's work was. He wished me luck." Max lapsed into silence.

I stared out the window as we zoomed past houses and cities.

"You would have liked Grandpa. He was down to earth and hated formal functions. To his last day, he drank whiskey and sat in his underwear to watch TV."

I chuckled.

"Yeah. Grandma came out to inform me of my new responsibility. She asked that I travel with her. The shipping business runs itself. I have to attend several meetings a year, and I get monthly reports, but I let the professionals actually run it." He chuckled. "Grandma didn't want me drinking like I was, so she used her 'I'm a sick old lady and have no one to take care of me' ploy. I took her up on the offer." Max shrugged again.

"And then you had all of those single women wanting to marry you."

His head snapped to look at me. "Yeah. I'm rich and single. When Grandma dies, I stand to inherit a whole lot more. And they only had two kids, Uncle Levit and Mom. Being an only child, I'll get half of the Grasicolli empire when Mom passes away. It skips Dad, though he'll never have to worry about money." Max shook his head. "All of those ladies were only after the money, believe me. I see it all the time with my cousins."

"Really?"

"Take Phillip. He's been married twice. It's been three years since his last marriage. So, he should be moving on to number three soon. He sleeps around a lot as far as I know. So does his wife. Even when they divorce, she'll get enough alimony to never have to work a day in her life."

I contemplated that. I bet it was hard, not knowing if the person you loved loved you for yourself or for your money. "I bet it's tough."

"Tough?"

"Not knowing if a woman wants you or just your money."

"Yeah. Even Clare was dating me for the money. I proposed to her because I thought she loved me. Before she answered, she asked about my future, and how long I was going to be a cop. It was then that I realized she was also after my money. We parted as friends."

I glanced at Max. The bitterness in his voice was obvious. "I'm sorry."

"For what?"

"All us gold-digging wenches."

Max started laughing.

I smiled. I liked making him happy.

"What would I do without you to make me laugh?"

"Find some other nut case to entertain you." I leaned over and kissed him on the lips as he drove. I moved back because the seat belt was uncomfortable like that, but left my hand on his upper thigh.

"I love eating nuts," Max said with sexy look in his eye.

I groaned at him. I massaged his thigh in circles. We travelled the rest of the way in silence.

***

I was standing on the deck near the pool area of the house. John called back, and I relayed the information to him concerning everything we had learned tonight. I was just finishing up when Max walked out with two drinks and the photo in hand. He had put it in an envelope.

Max handed me the drink first then sat down at the table near me. "Here's the photo. It digitized pretty well."

"Thanks." I took the envelope and gave him a tongue in the mouth kiss. I pulled back. "John says he'll follow through on the information with Dad."

Max nodded with a sexy look.

I glanced around the windows facing the pool. "Is everyone gone?"

"Why?"

"Skinny dipping." I nodded toward the pool.

Max glanced to it, then looked at me with desire in his eyes. He looked toward the house then smiled. "I think Phillip is still here." He stood up and grabbed my hand. "How about moving this into the house?"

I smiled back and leaned into a deep and mouthwatering, loin tingling kiss. We stood still kissing, leaving the drinks, phone and envelope on the table. Max pulled me toward the house, still not breaking the kiss. Two steps later we were near the side of the pool, and Max's hand moved to fondle my rear.

I pulled back and gave him a smile.

"What?"

Holding onto his shirt, I leaned away from him then with a little push, fell into the pool. He grabbed at me to stop my fall, then realized that I had done it intentionally. He smiled, laid his phone on the concrete and followed me into the pool.

I was deep in the pool and the lights were off. I came up to find Max emerge near me. We both cleared our faces with a shake, then continued kissing. Max slowly moved us along the edge of the pool toward the shallower end.

I was running my hand through his wet hair and beard as we kissed. My legs were wrapped around his waist. The pool water was warm and his hands were massaging my back.

132

When we reached the shallow end where there was a set of stairs, Max leaned on me. I was half submerged in the water. His eyes looked deeply into mine as he massaged other parts of my body. "I think we should take this inside."

Grabbing my hand, he led me out of the water and to the table where I gingerly picked up the envelope by the corner and my phone. He pulled me toward the house grabbing his phone enroute. Right before we entered the house he gave me another earth shattering kiss.

"I missed this." His voice was husky.

"Me too."

***

The next morning I was once more seated by the pool talking on the phone. I had a glass of juice with me and a piece of toast. My one pill was taken, and now I could take the rest in my pocket. "What did Dad say?"

"He found some of his notes. He's still looking for his case book. He thinks it's in a different box in the basement." Rich paused as he took a drink of something. "Good idea, Mel. When John called last night, I was amazed that we didn't think of it sooner."

I chuckled. "Yeah, me too." I looked up to see movement out of the house. I expected Max, but it was Phillip instead. He walked with purpose toward me.

"Do you still have the picture?"

"Yeah. I'll bring it with me."

"John told me last night that you are making a bigger picture of the two Mexican couples in thanks. I think that's a great idea."

"I think he got his money's worth."

Phillip motioned to sit next to me.

I nodded. "So, I'll see you tomorrow. I have one more day with Max, then I'll be free again to do your bidding."

Rich chuckled. "Take it easy, Sis."

"Sure." I hung up the phone and looked at Phillip. He had a strange look in his eyes. "Yes?"

"I was just wondering how long the two of you were staying here at the house?"

"We're leaving late today. Why?"

"I'm having a party tonight and, well, I was hoping..." Phillip leaned back to look at me with leering eyes.

I narrowed my eyes at him. "We'll be gone."

He smiled a wolf grin. "Last night I saw Max give you an envelope."

"Yeah. So?" I took a drink of my juice.

Phillip's eyes stared at my lips then swung down to the tank top I was wearing.

I watched his eyes roam over me.

"I saw the two of you in the pool." Phillip's wolf grin got bigger. "Max is one of the lesser relations in the family. He was a cop, you know." The way he said 'cop' was with sarcasm.

"And what's wrong with that? I know a lot of cops."

Phillip stood up and moved next to the table. "I bet you do. He knows just where to find... your kind of people."

I stood. My anger rising at the way he was demeaning Max. "And just what do you mean by that?"

"Max was even a waiter at one point. He has a taste for... lesser things." There was a pause. "Some people will do anything for money."

"Are you calling me a hooker?" I was more amused than angry.

"If the shoe fits." He leered again. "I have made love to some of the most beautiful women in the world. I would be glad to give you a lesson in more expensive tastes. Max is... common."

My anger exploded, and I swung on Phillip. My right hand connected with his face, and I felt a crunch in my fist. I watched as he fell back on the ground, blood spurting everywhere.

I pulled back my leg to follow up with a good kick to the side when I was grabbed from behind, my arms pinned. I struggled with this new threat.

"Mel, calm down."

I felt the volcano of anger spill out and dissipate rapidly. I took a breath. He released me slowly; apparently he wasn't sure that I wouldn't go after Phillip again.

Max turned me around as he looked at Phillip moaning on the ground holding his nose. "What is going on here, Mel?"

I took another breath. "Nothing. Phillip made some rude comments, and he needed to be put in his place."

"My nose... my nose..." Phillip moaned from the ground. "Grab the bitch. Keep her until the cops can get her. I want that whore arrested."

Max swept down on Phillip and picked him off the ground by his shirt front. He held him inches from his face. Max growled, "Mel is not a whore. She's my girlfriend. And whatever you said to her to make her hit you, you apologize for. Now."

Phillip stared at Max in horror. His hands barely containing the gushing blood. "The bitch broke my nose."

Max didn't let go of his hold on Phillip but turned to me. "What did he say to you?"

I looked Max in the eye. I didn't want to hurt him and repeat what Phillip said so I shook my head. "That is between him and me."

Max narrowed his eyes but turned back to Phillip and shook him. "Apologize to Mel."

Phillip shook his head. "The bitch broke my nose."

Max shook him once more. "And I'll break your jaw if you don't apologize to Mel."

Phillip stared at Max for a long second. He mumbled an apology.

I gave him the evil eye.

Max didn't look at me. "Mel, go inside please. I want to talk with my cousin. Alone."

I turned and walked into the house shaking my hand. I could still flex it, so it probably wasn't broken. I turned at the door and saw that Max brought Phillip up to his face as he spoke. Then in a disgusted move, Max tossed his cousin back to the ground. After taking a deep breath, he headed toward the garage.

I moved into the kitchen and popped my remaining pills before grabbing another piece of bread. I had to take these pills with food or my stomach hurt. I chewed and swallowed. Max appeared at my side from a different hallway. "What did he say to you?"

I shook my head. "It's not important." I flexed my fist again.

Max grabbed my hand and examined it.

I peered out the back door onto the deck. "Where's Phillip? He needs to be seen by a doctor. I think I might have broken his nose."

Max was still moving the bones in my hands, not looking at me. "You did. I called for Clarence to take him to the hospital." Finally, he let go of my hand and moved to the fridge. After getting a bag and filling it with ice, he held it on my hand. His eyes caught mine. "Did he call you a whore?"

"He implied it, but that didn't matter." I drank my juice.

"Then what?"

"It's over. I think he learned his lesson."

"Maybe." Max seemed puzzled. "If it wasn't about him insulting you, then what? I want to know."

I looked him in the eyes. "All I'll tell you is that it wasn't an insult to me." I kissed him on the lips and taking his hand off mine, walked away holding the bag.

Max followed me down the hall and into the rooms we were staying in. He sat on the bed while I fished a clean polo out of the suitcase one handed.

I could tell my knuckles were swelling. "Would you mind helping me with the shirt?"

"Mel, you are a most confusing woman. I'll never figure you out."

"Good." I smiled as I began to pull at the tank top.

Max stood up and moved the shirt over my head. He leaned in to kiss me, but I backed up. Max looked at me in surprise. "Why? We have plenty of time until your appointment."

"I want to go somewhere first." I held out the green polo shirt.

Max grabbed it. He put it over my head and pulled it down. Before getting it all the way down, he leaned in and kissed the top of the scar over my right breast. He stood back up and kissed me quickly on the lips.

I looked into his eyes. He had the same look he always gets when he tells me he loves me, but this was the third time he had looked at me that way and not said it.

I gathered the rest of the paperwork that I brought with me for the appointment. I figured the doctors would fax my records from the accident, but I wanted to make sure that Changri saw all of the injuries

I had sustained. Jason and company had gotten copies of my medical records for the still pending lawsuit. I had made copies of theirs before leaving Maryland and returning to Quincy.

Max grabbed the bundle and my other hand. "You are one crazy woman."

***

The morning seemed overcast, but it was probably just my feelings. Max was silent as he drove into the narrow entrance of the cemetery. The trees formed a canopy over the road. I pointed which way to go, and with only one misdirection, we finally stopped. I got out and stood by the car. I swallowed several times before actually walking away. As I moved among the tombstones, I felt the pain increase tenfold. By the time I stopped it was almost as painful as when I first heard the news.

I squatted down by the tombstone. With a gentle rub, I touched the headstone and traced the engraved letters. I laid the small bouquet of flowers near it.

I let the tears flow down my face untouched. The hurt was like the Grand Canyon. I hoped that one day it wouldn't tear so hard at my heart.

"I didn't get to tell you that night, but I love you."

I stood up and stared at the grave. My eye flicked to the tombstone next to his. It was Craig's. We had bought the plots a long time ago. I used mine to bury my son. I once more touched my son's memorial.

"Good bye, Robbie. Rest in peace, son."

I took a deep breath and turned away. The tears made the entire graveyard a blurry mass. I threaded my way across the turf, wiping my eyes.

When I looked up, Max was watching me with a gentle look on his face, one of understanding and caring. I moved to stand in front of him.

Max stood up from his lean on the car as I approached. He cocked his head to the side and with a compassionate expression, pulled me into his chest. He hugged me tight, not saying a word.

We stood that way for some time. Finally, I glanced at my watch. We needed to get going. "Thanks."

He didn't say anything but nodded. With an arm around my waist, he opened the car door and motioned me in. He closed the door then rounded the car.

I noticed that he gave one last look in the direction of the graves, then hopped into the car. Neither of us spoke until we reached Johns Hopkins.

Chapter 10

"So the whole Addison clan is going to be here?" Max asked as we drove to my parent's house. It was a large ranch style house with full basement. It was on a large lot which made the property look huge. A three car unattached garage stood by the alley with parking lot adjacent.

"All except Teresa and her fiancé. They live in Ohio." I slowed down to enter the alley. "So I think you've met everyone except Rich's family, Cam's girlfriend, and Mitch's girlfriend."

"Did Mitch finally settled down?"

I chuckled. "Probably not. I don't even know if Tina will be here. Same with Nancy, Cam's live-in."

"You're a lot happier." Max squeezed my arm and kissed my hand.

"Thanks again for pushing up the appointment. I don't know what I would have done for three weeks." I pulled into the parking lot to find it full. We were the last to arrive. I stopped the Jeep and gave Max a kiss.

"You're more than welcome. Money can't buy a lot of things, but it can help sometimes." He exited the vehicle to see Rich and Cam talking in the backyard. A small toddler, that they were ignoring, was running between them, and a little girl ran down the sidewalk to greet us.

"Aunt Mel... Aunt Mel... Look what I got." She ran holding up a small package.

I smiled at Max who looked uncomfortable. I waved at Rich and squatted down to the girl. "What did you get, Lizzie?"

The girl glanced at Max but dismissed him immediately, focusing on me. "It's new Pony Treasure stuff. I found this at Wal-Mart and Mom let me buy it. It matches the stuff you brought from California. See. Here's the big pony and here's the food and here's the stable."

"Wow." I looked into the box. Out of the corner of my eye I saw Max head over to Rich and Cam. "I bet it cost a lot of money." I stood up and walked with her to the group.

"Just a little, but I bought it with my birthday money."

Justin stopped playing between the grown-up's legs and ran for me. He held his hands up, smiling. He was only one and a couple of months. I scooped him up into my arms and walked toward the three men, with Lizzie still telling me about her new toys.

When we reached the group, Lizzie decided to go off and play. She disappeared into the house. I tickled Justin in the belly and he laughed and squirmed in my arms. I laughed and set him down. He immediately held up his arms again.

Rich shook his head. "Justin, go play."

"Diaper," I mentioned to Rich.

"Go find Mommy. You need a diaper change." He patted his son on the bottom as the boy toddled into the house.

Max accepted the beer Cameron offered him, but I shook my head. In actuality, I couldn't drink alcohol for at least three weeks, maybe longer. The new medication I was on was adversely affected by it.

"So, how was this mysterious event that you needed to go on?" Rich asked with a sly look at Cam. Both my brothers smirked.

"No mystery. Where's Dad? Did he find his case book?"

Rich nodded. "Yeah. John and I have been working on it today." He paused. "Ralph Zimmerman called earlier with a thanks. The nanny service you hired to watch his kids came right on time."

I smiled. Max had done that too. When we found out from the doctors that I was not to be around sick people, I called Ralph and found out that one of his kids was just getting over the flu. Max nixed my idea to babysit and hired the nanny service. "Good."

Dad walked up with a large smile on his face. He always liked Max and I'm sure was happy that he was back. "Hey Dad, do you remember a Martinez Tanto?"

140

"Only because I just saw his name in my old case book. He worked for the Hessors, didn't he? A grounds keeper."

"Yeah. He asked me to pass along to you…" I passed along the compliment. I could see it pleased Dad.

It wasn't long and Cam's girlfriend, Nancy, stepped out on the deck to let us know Mom wanted us. I had asked Mom to gather everyone tonight. I wanted to tell them all at once so my phone wouldn't ring off the hook tonight. She loved getting the whole family together.

Rich and Dad talked a little more, while Cam, Max and I walked into the house. Cam kissed Nancy as we entered the house, and I saw Max taking in the kitchen.

I had always thought Mom's kitchen was big. Growing up it was my favorite room. And it used to seem big even with the whole family in it. However, Mrs. Grasicolli's kitchen was huge compared to Mom's. I wondered what it would be like to have that big of a kitchen.

There was Mom, Nancy, Lizzie, Tina and Mitch, and lots of noise. Tina and Mitch were in the far corner, kissing. Cam and Nancy were doing the same near the door, while Gloria was just entering with Justin in tow. Mom was helping Lizzie with a drink.

Max glanced at me wide eyes and took a nervous drink of his beer.

I leaned closer. "What's wrong?"

"There's… never mind. I'll tell you later." He nodded with a smile at Mitch, who gave a head bob back to him, and went back to flirting with Tina.

I grabbed his hand. As we walked over toward Mom, Lizzie scooted between us with a quick 'excuse me.' Max lifted our hands to let her pass. "Mom, you've met Max, right?

She smiled. "Of course. At the hospital when you and Rich were hurt." She handed him a spatula. "You look like a man that can cook. Can you check the chicken on the grill? Thanks." She hurriedly turned to work on a pot of corn on the cob on the stove. She spoke over her shoulder at Max, "Just check it and let me know. If it needs more BBQ sauce just yell and, I'll send…" She raised her voice a bit, "…Mitch out with it."

"Yeah, yeah," Mitch replied, not even looking up from his flirting.

Max stood looking at the spatula as though he'd never seen one before.

I chuckled. "Better do as Mom says." I patted his butt.

Still looking shocked, he headed out onto the back deck. Cam chuckled too. It wasn't long, and Mom put me to work too. I was assigned to set the table. I gathered up Nancy and Gloria to help. By the time I made it back into the kitchen, Max was back inside.

This time Mom handed him five hot dogs for the grill. "The little ones won't eat chicken."

He glanced at me with a puzzled look but headed back outside.

By the time I finished my job, I escaped the kitchen to find Max in conversation with Dad and Rich on the deck. He closed the grill and laid the spatula on the side counter of the grill. A car pulling up in the crowded parking lot caught my attention. It was John's silver Mustang. He smiled as he walked up to the deck. "Got a minute?"

I nodded, and Rich said sure.

John opened his mouth to speak when Mom stepped out onto the deck. "Max dear, how is the chicken?"

"It's done, Mrs. Addison," Max said with a smile. "The hot dogs will be done in a minute too."

She handed him a platter. "Good. Put it on here and bring everything in. Hi, John."

"Dottie," John said with a smile.

"Come in and get washed up all of you... You too John. You may as well stay." With that, she headed inside.

John open and closed his mouth, slightly stunned. "I guess I'm staying. I have information on the young couple, but we can talk after dinner. Dottie wouldn't like us holding up the meal." John turned to Max. "Don't fight her. Just jump and say yes, ma'am. She's worse than any drill sergeant."

We all laughed as we slowly moved into the house. Max waited for me at the door with the meat platter. As everyone was assembling in the kitchen, he leaned into me and whispered, "Is she always this pushy?"

"Only when she wants something or is in charge of something. She likes you or she would have made you wait outside with Dad and

Rich." I winked. "She never lets anyone help her cook, even on the grill, unless you're special."

"Are all of your family gatherings this…"

"Confusing? Congested?"

He nodded as Mom called for him.

"Max? Is that all of the grilled meat?"

Dad chuckled as he passed. "You'll have to tell him about the Carl incident."

Max gave me a puzzled look as he headed to Mom's side. "Yes, Mrs. Addison."

Mom looked at him with a puzzled look. "What's this? Don't believe a word Mel tells you about me. And it's Dottie." She smiled. "Go ahead and put that on the table in there." She pointed to the dining room. "Mel… Mitch, you too. Get over here you lazy boy…"

I headed over and got handed the platter of corn on the cob and followed Max into the big dining room. Mitch followed shortly with the mashed potatoes and gravy. Soon Dad entered with potato salad and coleslaw.

Max looked at the table then back at me. "Your mom did all this?"

"Yeah. She loves to cook."

"Max!"

The face Max made was precious—little boy worried, mixed with a date meeting the parents for the first time kind of look.

The others were chuckling already. John spoke from the other side of the table. "Seems Dottie forgot about me."

"John!"

"Or not. Coming Dottie," John said obediently and followed a chuckling Max into the kitchen.

Soon we were all seated at the table, including Rich's kids.

Max seemed uncomfortable as we bowed our heads and Dad said grace. The noise intensified as food was passed around. Max seemed overwhelmed for a few seconds then settled down and dug in with the rest of us.

I took only a little bit on my plate. I wasn't hungry, and the new meds had taken the last of my appetite, but I had to eat something or

Mom would kill me. I smiled at Max as the conversation at the table was noisy and filled with laughter.

"Come on, Mel. Pass the potato salad. Stop hogging it," Cam said from the other side of the table.

I glanced at the bowl sitting in front of Max who reached out for it. I lightly slapped his hand. "Na uh. Manners, Cam. Nancy, you need to teach him better."

Nancy laughed.

Cam made a face at me, then he smiled. "Besides, it's not for me. Nan wants some."

"Oh no, Cam. Not today. I'm back on my diet. And I've already eaten too much. He wants it Mel." Nancy sat shaking her head with a smile, as though she knew how we siblings acted around each other.

"Diet? Again? Nancy dear, you are just right," Mom interjected into our conversation. "And Cam use your manners, we have guests."

"Who?" Cam looked around the table.

"Max," Mom said giving Cam the evil-Mom-eye. Rich and Mitch both snorted. "And John."

"John's here all the time. He's family. And Max..."Cam smiled at Max. "Shoot, as much as everyone used to talk about him..."

"Really?" Max asked me.

I shrugged.

Mom pointed at Cam. The message was clearly understood by all.

Cam smiled a fake smile. "Fine. Melissa my lovely, *older* sister would you please, if it isn't too much trouble, pass Mom's delicious potato salad down the table so that I can partake of it. Please and pretty please."

"But of course, since you asked so nicely." Instead, I passed it in the other direction. Laughter followed along with a napkin missile aimed at me but missed.

"Oh really?!" I crumpled up my napkin staring at Cam.

"Melissa Ann Elizabeth Addison."

"Not four names!" I laid my napkin down in fake guilt. "Oh yes, wouldn't want to hurt the *baby*." Another missile headed my way. Missed again. I laughed at Cam. He always was a bad shot.

"Cameron Justin Marcus Addison!"

He grinned at Mom. And when she wasn't looking, I tossed one of his napkin bombs back at him. Hitting him right in the face.

Max shook his head and went back to eating, but he was smiling.

And the battle continued whenever Mom wasn't watching. Mitch joined in. Lizzie tried to but was stopped by Gloria who kept giving us dirty looks. Rich ignored us. John kept passing me more napkins. Even Dad got into it by tossing one at Mom. That earned everyone a dirty look from her.

When the food was consumed and everyone was just talking and tossing things at each other, Mom stood up and looked around the table. Myself and my siblings all avoided her eyes, even John had learned. We knew she was searching for volunteers to help with clearing the table and passing out desert.

"Max, John, Tina and Nancy..." Mom announced. "Each of you grab some plates and bowls and help me clear the table."

Max stood up. I was already helping to gather stuff for the named 'volunteers' as were my siblings. Max gave me a smirk and headed in with his arms full of stuff. He soon returned for more. Finally, the table was cleared and dessert was served. The little ones were off playing a computer game.

Mom cleared her throat. "So Mel, you called this thing together."

I swallowed as everyone looked at me. "Yeah, but first Mitch has something he wants to say. Don't you turd-head."

"Okay, dog breath...Two things... First of all, I got a promotion at work. I made Detective."

The family congratulated him.

"And... I, uh... Well..."

"He finally did it," Rich said with a punch at Mitch's arm.

Max looked at me confused and I winked.

Mitch blushed. A very rare thing for him. He looked at Tina with a big grin on his face. "Yeah, she agreed to marry me."

Mom rushed over and kissed Tina who also blushed. Dad was beaming and gave Tina a kiss on the cheek.

After Mom sat down and the family quieted, Mom asked, "So, when am I getting more grandkids?"

Mitch once more smiled at Tina. "In about another seven months."

Mom's mouth dropped open.

The rest of the family laughed.

"Twins."

"Oh my God," Mom said putting her hand to her mouth. Now she rushed to Mitch and kissed him, then Tina again.

I chuckled. Max was just watching the interplay between family members. After more gushing and congratulations, the family settled down again. Mom looked at Max then expectantly at me.

I chuckled with a shake of my head. "Don't get any ideas."

Max looked at me then at Mom, then blushed.

The rest of the family laughed again.

"I'm afraid my news isn't quite as good as Mitch's, although it's still good news," I said taking a drink of my tea.

I felt Max's hand on my thigh give me an encouraging squeeze.

"So…" Dad said. The room got a lot quieter.

"Well, I've been battling an illness for some time. As you know, I've had trouble shaking this cold thing." I saw nods all around. "My immune system pretty much shut down for a while."

Mom sucked in a breath in fear.

I shook my head at her with a smile. "Not to worry. Corbet here in town was having trouble diagnosing it, so he sent me to John's Hopkins in Maryland. The appointment wasn't for three weeks, but Max called and got it moved up to yesterday."

Mom looked at Max with a new look in her eye. Max squirmed in his chair under her gaze.

"It turns out that following the car accident, I caught a very virulent bacterial infection that sort of lay dormant for a while."

"You were susceptible to any cold that came around since then," Mom said softly.

I nodded. "The drug that I was given in California activated it, they think. Anyway, the injury to my rib from the gun shot took longer to heal due to it and…" I paused looking down at the table. "I've had pneumonia four times since coming home from California."

Mom opened her mouth to speak. I could see the angry look in her eye. "How come—"

"I'm now on a really strong antibiotic that should cure the infection. The doctors at John's Hopkins are sure that in about four weeks I should be fully healed if I follow their orders."

"And those are?" Rich asked softly from the other side of the table.

"I'm not to be with anyone who is sick. No hospital visits. I'm not allowed to be in any smoky environments, or any place that has a lot of chemicals. Basically, I'm not to stress my lungs and body in any way. Also, no alcohol. It affects the drugs. So…" I looked around the table. "Overall, good news." I smiled.

The table was silent.

Max cleared his throat. "She's suppose to take it easy and get lots of rest." He glanced at me with a knowing look, as though he knew I would leave that part out.

"Will this be a life time thing or what?" Dad asked.

I looked up to see everyone concerned. "No. Once I get this cured, I should be okay. I may be more susceptible to colds and stuff than most people, but once my immune system kicks back in, they said I should be fine."

John sat back looking at the family members. "So, have you told Landry about this?"

"Yes. Jason was informed first thing. He has resubmitted papers to the court." I sighed. "That means that that particular lawsuit will drag out even more."

"So this is from the car accident? It was caused by that?" Mitch asked leaning forward.

I glanced at Max. "Mostly."

"Mostly?" Now Cam jumped in.

"Yeah."

Rich shook his head. "Out with it, Mel. There's more, isn't there?"

I nodded my head and glanced down at the table. Max reached out and patted my arm. I knew the whole family was watching. I looked up at Max and he inclined his head to the table.

I took a deep breath. "The doctors at John's Hopkins said that it was probably started by a sexually transmitted disease that I had two years ago. The original disease was cured by my drugs from the car accident, so I no longer need to worry about it. But the bacterial infection took hold then and just never developed until the drug interacted with it in California."

Mitch shook his head, his tone hardening. "So he was cheating on you?"

I gave a little nod of my head still looking at the table.

"Who was?" Mom asked confused. A beat later she continued, "You were married. Craig cheated on you?"

I did the nod thing again and looked up. "Yeah. I caught him once. And it wasn't the first time." I looked at Mitch, whose eyes had hardened. He had never liked Craig.

I shrugged. "It's over and there's no use in bringing it back up. The past is the past. I've moved on. And as soon as this infection goes away, I'll be cured."

Silence ruled for a few seconds.

Finally Mom spoke softly. "Well, then... thank you Max."

Max just looked at her.

"Mel would never have told us if you hadn't forced her, not to mention helping her with moving the appointment up."

Max was now the center of attention, and he really seemed uncomfortable and embarrassed. "It was just... I like... well... I just wanted to help, Dottie."

Suddenly Mitch, Rich and John started laughing at the same time. I blushed, and the others joined in the mirth.

Mom clapped her hands for attention. "Okay then, the spawn need to do the dishes."

We kids groaned but headed to the kitchen. I leaned down and gave Max a kiss on the cheek. "I told you we did a lot of dishes."

Max chuckled and ended up talking with John on the deck. At one point, they were cornered by Mom. God only knows what they were talking about.

We were almost done with the dishes when Max walked into the kitchen to get another beer. He stopped as I scooted around him. I peeked out from around him, a huge smile on my face.

Mitch was advancing on us with towel twirled. "Come out. Don't hide behind Max. You started this."

Max laughed. With a quick move, he jumped out from in front of me.

I laughed and flicked Mitch with my towel. Mitch yelped and swung toward me with his. I used a move that Max had taught me and caught his towel in mine. With a snap of the wrist, his towel was mine. I grinned evilly at Mitch as I slowly moved toward him, spinning my towel.

"Mel… Mel… You wouldn't."

I smiled even more evilly. "You've already spawned. You can't use that as an excuse anymore, buddy boy."

Mitch covered himself with his hands still moving backward. He came up against Cam and pulled him around to use as a shield. That wouldn't stop me, and all of us knew it.

"Hey!" Cam called out. "Leave me out of this! Mel, I'm not in this fight." His hands dripped water onto the floor.

Rich stepped between us. "Could you two act like adults just once!"

I smiled at Mitch who grinned back. With an evil look at Rich, I tossed the towel back to Mitch. We grinned at each other.

Rich got a look on his face. "No way… Crap…" And he took off running out the back door.

Mitch and I were fast on his heels. I could hear Max laughing as we chased Rich down the sidewalk.

It wasn't too much later and John, Rich and I were gathered on the deck. Tina and Mitch had already left. Max was talking to Dad in the basement.

"Here's what my contact found out," John said. "The young couple are Madeline's sister and husband. Elizabeth and Martin Accard spent a lot of time with the Hessors prior to Horace's death. The year away was mostly spent in Mexico. I tracked the group as best I could after this long. Bart was born in Mexico City, Mexico. Elizabeth and Martin Accard are listed as his parents on the birth certificate."

Rich chuckled. "So technically Hessor is not an American citizen."

"Yes. He'll need to do the paperwork."

"Maybe Mitch can get him deported." Rich's smile bordered on evil.

"Doubt it," John replied.

"Still might be worth the effort."

149

"Why hide his birth parents? What's the reason?" I asked after drinking the last of my tea.

Both men shrugged.

"Drugs?"

"Probably." Rich finished off his beer. "Doesn't matter. We did our job."

"I'll inform Hessor in the morning," John said and stood up. He passed Max coming out the door. I could hear John thanking Mom for the meal.

"Ready to head home?" Max asked.

"What? Is it past my bed time?"

"Remember what the doctor said. Lots of rest."

Rich snorted. "He doesn't know Mel. Orders never work."

"And she doesn't know me." Max gave me a serious look. "Let's go. Time to rest." He grabbed my empty glass and handed it to Rich. "I've already said our good-byes." He held out his hand.

I sighed and stood. Having Max boss me around felt both smothering and good all at the same time.

Rich stood too. "Wow! Someone who can tell Mel what to do and she listens."

I punched Rich in the arm. Hard. He yelped and rubbed his deltoid. Then he grinned. "Shut up." I threatened to punch him again, but he quickly moved away.

"Bully." Max chuckled and followed me off the deck. As we walked down the sidewalk to the parking lot, he took my hand. With a smile he kissed me. "I know you're just humoring me because you'll do what you want, but you do need to rest."

I smiled. "As long as we know who is in charge."

"Yeah. Your Mom."

***

We lay in bed later that night relaxing. I was curled up comfy on Max's chest. He rubbed my arm.

"Your family is… nice."

I chuckled. "Mom likes you."

150

"I thought just the opposite, with the way she kept picking on me."

"Nah. That's mom's way of bringing you into the family."

"What was that your dad mentioned... the Carl incident?"

"Teresa's fiancé. The first time T brought him home with her from college, before they were engaged, Mom cornered him similar to how she did you tonight. Carl was a nervous wreck. He dropped the plate of burgers on the deck and then spilled wine on the table cloth. He has since been banned from helping with 'things.' Not good in Mom's estimation. She likes helpers, little troopers to work for her around meal time."

"John seems like he's been accepted."

"Yeah. Mom really likes John. The first time Rich brought him there, I hear it was yes, ma'am and no, ma'am. Really impressed her. Now anytime she can, she invites him to dinner. Thanksgivings and Christmases are a sure thing. He rarely goes to visit his own family."

"Where?"

"I don't really know. St. Louis, I think. Maybe. He has a lot of connections there. Only one time did he mention them and that was to say he was kicked out of the family."

Max thought about that. He leaned down and kissed my forehead.

"What about the information he told us about Bart? What do you make of that?"

Max shook his head. "So the young couple were traveling with the Hessors when Bart was born. And she is Madeline Hessor's younger sister and Bart's mom, according to records. I wonder why Madeline is hiding it?"

"But then again, it seems silly to hide his birth anyway. And another thing, I wonder what Horace Hessor died of?"

"What?"

"Bart's uncle, Madeline's husband. How did he die? I thought about that the other day in Maryland sitting on Hernandez's porch. Isn't it a little strange that he died only four months after Bart was brought to Quincy? I wonder if his records are still available?"

"I don't see the connection?"

"Maybe there isn't one." I looked up at Max. "Just a nutcase talking."

Max laughed and kissed me on the lips. "A very beautiful nutcase."
I blushed.

"I mean it."

"Hey, what was going on with you at the house anyway. You almost looked scared." Changing the subject away from us made me feel better.

Now Max blushed. "I've never been around so many people that seemed to care about each other… My family get togethers, which are few and far between, consist of seeing who can drink the other under the table and cutting each other up with rude comments."

I gave him a look of disbelief.

"Okay maybe I exaggerate a little, but not much. Your family is so… accepting and loving. It… I don't think I have even been around people quite like that. It threw me for a minute or two."

"Or half the night."

Max chuckled. "It was different. Now, my dear woman, let me show you something…" He leaned over and began kissing me. I knew where we would end up.

***

The next morning I was talking on the phone when Max walked out from his shower. He was dressed in a forest green t-shirt and khaki shorts. My eyes wandered up and down his body. His bare feet made him even more sexy. *Man, he is yummy!*

Max chuckled and shook his finger.

"Yeah, and what did the coroner say about it?"

After retrieving orange juice from the fridge he sat down puzzled. He pointed at the phone.

"The records only show that it was a blunt object. Not found at the scene. Crime scene photos show a weird looking tool mark on the skull."

"Really! And no one thought that was odd?"

"Anyway to get murdered is odd, Mel." Mitch's voice had an amused sound.

I chuckled. "Yeah, put that way, I guess. Do you think Dad might know about this?"

"He might. His name isn't in the records, so it wasn't his case, but I'm sure he had a passing knowledge of it. If he still remembers." There was a pause. "You aren't going to let this go, are you? You're going to keep digging now, huh?"

"I'm just curious."

"Yeah, right." He sighed. "Look…" He lowered his voice. "If I can, I'll make a copy and bring it to the office, but I didn't do this. Got it?"

"Sure. Thanks, Mitch." I hung up as Max leaned over and kissed me. "Good morning."

"Yeah, a really good morning. This morning you were… amazing."

I laughed. I popped my two morning pills. "You inspire me."

"Where did you learn to do that with your tongue?"

I merely smiled.

"What's up with Mitch?"

"I had him pull Horace Hessor's file. As Rich remembered, it is still filed as unsolved."

"Murder? I thought it was a botched robbery?"

I shrugged. "Mitch is bringing it by the office today. Unofficially. But Dad might remember more about it. Mitch says it wasn't his case but…" I smiled. "I also have my contact at the library finding me the old newspaper clippings on his death. There has got to be something there."

"Why are you still concerned with old man Hessor's death?"

I hesitated. "I'm betting this is drug related, including Horace Hessor's death. But why? And where did the other two end up? Are they alive? Or were they killed too? And is Madeline behind all of this? And why?"

"Why does it matter now that Hessor has his answer?"

"I'm curious."

"Tiger, if they couldn't solve Hessor's murder all those years ago, I doubt you'll get a fresh lead on it now." Max was giving me his 'I know better than you look.'

"I just want to see the reports. What harm will it do?"

Max sighed softly, apparently just giving in.

I smiled as my phone rang. "Hello?"

"Hi. Is this Mel Addison?"

"Yes. Who is this?"

"Marris Cletonski. Do you remember me from the other day?"

"Yeah. Al Herdsman's former secretary."

Max perked up.

"I got to thinking more and more about Brady Carson. So, I headed to Al's garage. His wife is getting ready to sell their house, and she talked to me several months ago about what to do with Al's old records. I didn't even think of this when you were here. Anyway, I went over there and rummaged through the boxes."

My eyes met Max's. I knew my eyes widened in hope. Max's face got puzzled. I held up a finger. "And?"

"I found the old file. Would you like to see it?"

"Absolutely. Can I come over right now?"

"That's why I called." I could hear her smile.

I glanced at my watch. "I can be there in about fifteen minutes. Is that good for you?"

"Sounds good."

"Thanks, Mrs. Cletonski." I hung up and relayed the information to Max.

He chuckled. "Lucky. You are very lucky." He stood and gave me another breath stopping kiss. "Give me a minute."

As he hurried away, I moved to the counter to put the two pill bottles away and slightly twisted as I reached for the cabinet. A pain laced through my chest. I gasped for breath for a second, grabbing the counter in response. Then it went away. *What was that?* I rubbed my chest. *If it happens again, I'm definitely calling Changri's office.* By this time, Max had his shoes on and ready to go.

***

I studied the file with Max reading over my shoulder. Brady Carson had been bailed out by a lady whose name was Virginia Nefort. I turned my head slightly, staring at the floor.

Max was watching me, waiting.

I looked up at Marris. "Thanks. Can I keep this file for a few days? I promise to return it. I'd like my associates to see this."

She shrugged. "Sure. I don't think Al will care."

After we got in the car, Max turned to me. "The snooping sneak strikes again. What did you see in there?"

"What do you mean?"

"I saw that look. What did you see that I didn't?"

I shook my head. "The lady's name. I've seen it before, but where? I want to run it in the databases and look in my other files. I know I've seen that name."

Max said nothing the entire trip to the office.

I was glad because I was running the name through my own data base in my head. I frowned, it was not coming to me.

Max's hand on my leg startled me after we parked in front of the office. "Let it rest, Tiger. It'll come."

I huffed and got out. As I stepped down, another pain shot through my chest, causing me to pause and gasp again.

Max was by my side in a second. "Mel? What's wrong?" His hands were on my back and waist.

I shook my head as the pain passed. "Not here." I glanced around. "Mel…Tell me."

"A pain in my chest. It happened this morning too." I rubbed the right side as I stood there. "It's gone now. I'm fine."

The cold, steely look was back.

"No, I am." I hopefully gave him a confident smile.

"Mel…" His tone was a definite warning.

"Look, don't make a scene. Rich will make one call and the whole city will come down on me. Smothered again. Just let it go for now."

"I want you checked out."

"Later." I moved to go past him, but he held me firm. I looked into his eyes and they were granite. "I'm calling Changri when I get in. Just don't cause a scene."

His eyes stayed hard, but he let go of me. "Don't mess around with this, Mel. You will call, so help me God."

"I will." I moved around him and put on a smile for Pam who was watching us from inside. The door closed behind me as Max stood on the sidewalk his back to the window.

Pam nodded with a questioning look toward him.

I glanced back. "Men!"

Pam grinned as the door opened. "Good morning, Max."

"Hi, Pam." He seemed back to his old self, but his eyes gave him away. They flicked to the hall and back to me.

"Rich or John in?"

Pam shook her head. "Out. Do you need them?"

"No. I just had a question. Thanks." I headed back to my office, Max at my heels. When I turned around, Max was shutting the door.

He pointed at the phone.

I grimaced as I sat. When I twisted around in the chair to get at the file cabinet, the pain struck again. I bent over in pain.

Max moved fast. "You're going to the hospital. Now."

"No. Wait. I think I know what this is." I sat back and breathed several times.

His face puckered in anger. "Don't pull this with me."

I held up my hand. "Seriously." I looked him in the eyes. "I think this is a muscle spasm. It feels the same, only I'm used to them in back not in front."

"From?"

"Changri mentioned that my muscles on the right side were very weak, remember? He suggested several exercises. I started this morning. I think I over did it." I was still gazing into his eyes. "Honestly."

He visibly relaxed and moved back to the chair.

I picked up the phone as I dug into my pocket for my wallet. Quickly I dialed Changri's office. The doctor was busy, but after being on hold for several minutes I finally spoke to the nurse.

I described the pain and she also thought it was a pulled muscle. She suggested several things to help ease the pain. The thing that convinced her was that it always occurred when I was twisting or turning. If they were still affecting me tomorrow, she suggested going to my regular doctor. I thanked her and hung up.

"She's convinced it's just a muscles spasm too."

Max's expression didn't change.

I smiled.

He relented a little. "If it doesn't go away, you are getting checked."

I frowned. I didn't like to be bossed around or told what to do.

"Get mad at me. I don't care, Mel. If it continues, I'll take you there myself. Even if I have to drag you kicking and screaming." He pointed at me, his expression still stone.

"Fine." I huffed slightly and turned on the computer. I ran the data bases for the new name but came up with zip.

Mitch showed up and handed me the file. "These are copies. Officially, I wasn't here."

I nodded as I opened it. "Max, did you hear someone?"

Max chuckled along with Mitch, who quickly left. "Well?"

"Horace Hessor's file."

He scooted his chair around the desk as I opened the file. I spread the old police report out. We spent a few minutes perusing the paperwork. After a while he leaned back in his chair.

"What?"

"Jimmied window. Missing statues and money. That's why it was ruled a botched burglary."

"I hear a but in your voice."

He smiled. "But… no fingerprints besides the Hessors' and their hired help. All of the workers have alibis. They all had the night off. Madeline, and the sister and brother-in-law all stick to the same story. No footprints after the rainy night."

"Someone had doubts."

"Yeah. Definitely suspicious," Max said. "That's why it was never officially closed. He pointed at the open file. "Someone didn't believe the stories."

"Hmmm."

"Let it go. You can't solve this one." Max leaned forward and gave me a gentle kiss on the lips, just a light touch with the right amount of spark. His phone rang and he looked at the front. "Gotta take this." Quickly he left the office answering the phone.

I sighed and gathered up paperwork. As I stuffed it into the file, I noticed an envelope. Curiosity is a bad habit of mine. It's gotten me into more trouble than my mouth and attitude combined. I opened it and saw that Mitch had made photo copies of the crime scene photos too. Not great copies, but I still studied them.

The majority of them were of the house and room where Hessor had been found dead. The last one was of the injuries to Hessor. There was a clear picture of the fatal wound. I stared at it. Mitch had been right, it was a weird type of injury. The autopsy photo showed a definite square injury.

I dug into the file again and pulled out the autopsy report. I had only given it a passing glance before. Now I read it in detail.

Blood alcohol high. Not unusual according to the police file. The hired help said that both the Hessors and the other couple drank heavily. Other drugs in his system. The list matched his prescription drugs. Blunt trauma to the back of the head. Obvious. The wound was a two by three inch rectangle. Right over the brain stem. The person hit Horace as he sat in his office chair. Died instantly. The person was estimated to be approximately five nine. The coroner had no idea of the type of weapon.

My eyebrows raised as I read a little farther down. Horace had had sex shortly before death, there was still semen and vaginal fluid in his pants. I paused and paged back to the police reports and interview notes. Horace and Madeline slept in separate bedrooms and, according to the help, hadn't gotten along in over three years. The marriage was in name only.

My phone rang. "This is Mel."

"Hi, it's Judy." Like I wouldn't recognize her voice. "I sent the news articles about Horace Hessor's death like you asked. Should be in your email."

"Thanks. Decide where and when for lunch." We hung up, and I turned on my computer. I quickly read through my email and her articles. They didn't help much. Several I just passed over since they weren't about Hessor's death but articles about Elizabeth and Martin Accard. They were my next place to investigate.

I sat back and thought as Max walked into the room. He slid into the chair and watched me.

"What is the snooping sneak thinking about now?"

"I don't know. Something is tickling my brain. Something small."

"Talk it out. Usually helps."

"Okay. Hessor died of blunt force trauma to the head." Max nodded. "But no weapon was found."

"Murderer took it with him."

"No footprints."

"Yes. Puzzling or he stayed on the concrete."

"True. The coroner had no idea what the weapon was."

"Could be anything. Almost anything can be used to hit someone over the head."

I shook my head. "Fatal injury was a rectangle two by three inches."

Max leaned back too. "Hmmm." He rubbed his chin in thought.

I pulled my eyes away from him because it was so sexy watching him stroke his beard. "Rectangle. What would be something that had a rectangle on the end?"

Max thought for all of one minute then stopped and shook his head. "You drew me into this. Let it go."

"It's just a mental exercise. I don't really think that I can solve it." I didn't mean those words, but I saw that he believed me. I think.

He grabbed a book off the printer stand and with a smirk and tilt of his head, opened it. It was a textbook from the private detective school that I was taking online. That particular book was a listing of websites that might be useful in doing skip traces. I knew it was boring, but Max was concentrating hard on it anyway.

After a couple minutes of watching him 'read' the book and me just sitting and thinking, I chuckled at him. "Great reading, huh?"

"Didn't know there were online classes."

"Yeah, the business is paying for it. It's part of my internship with the guys. I have another two years before I can call myself a private detective."

Max hefted the book. "There's some good sites in here. Do you use this often?"

"John does most of the skip tracing. I help occasionally with tracking…" I was staring at the book. A book is rectangular. I briefly closed my eyes as my brain kicked into gear with the tickle. I held up my hand to stop Max from talking. I had heard him take a breath. "Holy moly." I grabbed the photos of the crime scene again.

"What?"

"Just a minute…" I spread out the photos of the room and studied the tables and all of the decorations on the table. "I wonder… He did say…"

"What? Who said what?"

I grabbed the phone and rummaged through the paperwork on the desk for a number. "I just thought of something." Finally I found the number and was dialing as Max sat back down in front of me.

"What? The tickle?"

I nodded. "Hi, is Bart around."

Max's expression darkened and his eyes narrowed.

"Thanks. No, tell him it's Mel Addison. I have a question for him. It's important and it won't take long… Thanks." I shook my head at Max. "Stop."

He sat back and crossed his arms. "John should be making this call. It will only encourage Hessor."

"John can't make this call because it's something Bart won't talk about to anyone."

His expression deepened in it's anger.

"Look, come over and listen at my ear." I motioned him over. He got there just as Bart answered the phone.

"Hello, Mel." The tone was openly sexual. "Tired of the ex-cop?"

I ignored him and Max's stiffening posture near me. "Look Bart, I've got a serious question, and I'd like an honest answer."

"Sure."

"Remember when we were teens and you had me over to your house? It was the night before the infamous trip to the island."

"Hmm… Vaguely."

"Vaguely?"

"Okay, I'm lying. I remember it vividly. You were wearing that green halter top that let your hard nipples show. The cut off jeans were tight enough to let me see your complete butt. It was hot." He paused. "That vivid enough for you?"

Max growled.

I put my finger to my mouth. "Yeah. Listen. In your Aunt's den, there was a statue of a figure. I think it was a lady. You told me she owned it before you were born."

"Yeah. Aunt Maddie always loved that statue. She said it was her good luck statue. What about it?"

"Where is it?"

"Why?"

"Just answer the question."

There was a pause on the line where he was obviously thinking. "I'm pretty sure I put it in storage until she gets out next month. I know I still have it somewhere. I snuck it into my bag as the police took me to the foster house, after they arrested her. Again, why?"

"Was the statue holding something?"

"A book, if I recall correctly. Why?"

"Just something that has been bugging me. Did she always have it out when you were growing up?"

"Uh… Yeah. The first time I remember it was around seven or eight. I knocked it off the table and I thought she was going to have a fit. Luckily I didn't break it. It was her favorite statue of all time, that's why I took it with me to the foster home. Why?"

"Where was it before that?"

"I don't know." He paused to think. "Couldn't have been out on the table before, I just don't remember… Wait. I remember once she said she kept in the bank in the safety deposit box with her jewels. She almost took it back there when I knocked it off. Why?"

"Thanks for the information."

"Does this have something to do with my parents?"

"Maybe. I'm not sure." I heard a chuckle.

"Mel, you will forever be a mystery to me. Anyway, I need to go. I hope this information helped." There was a pause. "By the way, you wouldn't by any chance still have that green halter top, would you?"

"Go to hell, Bart." I hung up on him as he started laughing.

"What was that about?" Max asked moving back to the other chair.

161

"Look at the photo." I slid the old black and white photo to him.

He nodded. "Could be the shape of a book. What of it?"

"Tanto said that when everyone came back, Madeline and Horace were arguing all the time, over business among other things."

"So?"

"What if she clocked him upside the head with the statue? Her good luck statue? It's not in any of the photos." I motioned to the ones spread over the desk.

Max's expression turned condescending. "Tiger, I'm sure that the cops checked out all of the statues in the house."

"And if she had already gotten rid of the statue? Already put it away? Hid it."

"Okay. I'll play your 'what if' game. If she did, there is no way that you could prove any of it."

"Unless the book matches the statue."

"There is no way you are getting that statue from Hessor. I guarantee it," Max said with a finality to his tone.

"True." I frowned.

"Mel!" Pam's voice floated down the hall.

Max leaned back and opened the door without leaving his chair.

"Yeah?" I called to her.

"Line one. Your contact at the library."

"Thanks." I picked up the phone. "Judy?"

"Yeah. I asked my friend at Interlibrary Loan about the Hessors. She sent me some articles that she found. Some are different and from different sources than I found. I didn't know if you still needed more, but I sent them via email too."

"Won't hurt. Thanks" I hung up the phone.

"It was a good thought, the statue with the book but improvable."

John stuck his head in the doorway as he passed by.

"Hey, John…" Max called and hurried out of the room. I heard John's door close.

I perused the clippings anyway. Again, curiosity. Horace had been found in the living room of the house seated at his desk. We already knew this from the police reports. Everyone had an alibi. Madeline had been out with her brother-in-law and sister who were visiting. They had been at the nearby lake on a picnic. The house help had the day off, as did most of the ground's people too. Ava had taken Bart into town with her. And the windows had been jimmied.

Over time, the story slowly faded off of the front page of the newspaper, then from even the inside. The last clipping, two years after the incident, said that the lead investigator had retired, and the police still had no substantial leads.

I sat back and gave it some thought. *Where had the old investigator gone? Was he still alive?* I ran his name through the data bases to find that he had died four years ago. Dead end.

What about the young couple? John had tracked them to a small town outside of St. Louis. Martin Accard was still alive, but Elizabeth had died only a year after Hessor in a car accident. I dug into the data bases to look at her accident. Finally I found the back issues of the newspaper in St. Louis.

She had apparently been drinking and ran her car into a telephone pole. Died instantly. I stopped reading at that point. This was useless. The officials were satisfied, and why was I beating a dead horse? Bart was even satisfied with our findings. His lawyer was in touch with Martin, negotiating to do a DNA test to determine without any doubt that Martin Accard and Elizabeth Harding-Accard were his parents.

The case was closed.

I glanced at my watch. It had been over an hour since Max and John had sequestered themselves in his office. I wondered what was up with them. I was shutting down the site I was on when a snippet of the article caught my eye.

Elizabeth Accard had only been released from the mental hospital two days before the accident. She had been a resident of the hospital since their arrival in St. Louis. According to the paper at the time, she had been despondent over the death of her brother-in-law. An anonymous source said that she was pregnant with her first child. *What? First child! But she had given birth to Bart.*

My thoughts ran in circles, then lightning struck. I stood up, grabbed the file and headed to John's office. I knocked on the door, and when I entered Max and John were both silent. They were looking at me like I had interrupted some sort of high level meeting. I stood there staring at them as they stared at me.

"Yes?" John asked leaning back in his chair.

"I've been going over Horace Hessor's police case and doing some looking into the databases. I just found something... intriguing." I handed the police file to John. Max was sitting there almost lost in thought. I glanced at him then back to John.

"Where are you going with this, Mel?" John asked.

"Okay, it's a long shot, but just hear me out..." I paused to take a deep breath. This sounded even silly to me, but I wanted to get his opinion. "The two couples return from their stay in Mexico. Madeline and Horace are fighting like cats and dogs. Martin and Elizabeth are there too. Suddenly Horace is found dead in the house. Conveniently all of the help is on a day off. Tanto mentioned when Max and I were talking to him that the Hessors rarely gave them time off, usually demanded them to work over time. Why that day? The other three have alibis which are substantiated by each other. After Horace's death, Elizabeth gets put into a psycho ward because she is 'distraught' at Horace's death.

"Martin never held a job that I can find. Yet according to the data bases, he has always lived in expensive houses. He seems to never want for money, that I can find. Trips and nice cars, etc..."

"Okay."

"Elizabeth finally makes it out of the nut-farm, and according to an anonymous source, pregnant. She dies, conveniently, in a car accident. Both she and the baby are killed. Martin moves to a bigger house." I paused. I wasn't' really sure where this was going either.

"What does that have to do with anything?" Max chimed in.

"Wait. Let's play what if again... What if one of them, Madeline, killed Horace. They back up each other's story. She, according to the police, was the last to 'see' him that morning. It's in the police file." I pointed to the unopened file in his hand.

"Go on."

"They leave almost immediately after Horace's death and Elizabeth gets put in an insane asylum, to keep her quiet. I bet if we could get her records, she makes illusions to the killing. Anyway, when she gets out, she is killed by either Madeline or Martin."

"How was Horace killed?" John asked.

"Blunt trauma to the back of the head." Max informed him. "Police speculate a burglary gone bad, but there were unanswered questions. And they never found the murder weapon or the perp."

John looked puzzled.

"The missing piece here is…" I hesitated. "Don't tell Rich this…"

John tilted his head.

Max rolled his eyes.

"Right before Madeline was arrested, I went with Bart to their house. He left me in the den while he went to his room to get something. I wandered around looking at all of the expensive stuff. I was fascinated by a particular statue. A woman holding a book of some sort. I remembered Bart saying something like it was his Aunt's favorite good luck statue."

"Did you know that your dad was investigating the Hessors?" John asked with an air of 'I can't believe you.'

"Sort of. Anyway…" I made a hand motion to dismiss that part of the conversation.

John gave a disbelieving look at Max who nodded in agreement.

"Anyway, I called Bart and asked him about the statue…"

"You did what? I told you…"

I continued ignoring John, "He told me that Madeline had stored it for a number of years in her bank vault. That it was her favorite good luck statue. Bart snagged it as they took him away to the foster care system. Anyway, the pictures of Horace's fatal injury look similar to the book held by the lady, if I remember correctly."

"Where is the statue now?" John asked.

"Hessor still has it," Max answered him. "He's saving it for his Aunt's return."

"I still don't see where this is going, Mel?"

"What if Madeline killed Horace? Then Elizabeth is having problems with her part in the scheme, so they silence her by committing her to the nut farm. I'm sure that would be easy for a woman like Madeline Hessor to do. Martin gets 'kept' by Madeline as

165

she becomes the Queen of drugs in the area. When Elizabeth gets out, maybe she threatened to tell or something, she gets wacked by them. A car accident would be easy to do."

"And you think Martin killed his own kid?" Max asked.

"What if it wasn't Martin's kid? What if during the course of this, Elizabeth gets knocked up by someone at the nut farm? There's an anonymous source that said there were rapes at the nut farm." I paused as my mind was jumping way ahead. "What if Elizabeth isn't Bart's mom?"

"That anonymous source is probably very wrong, Mel," John instructed me. "Those kind of sources have to be taken with a grain of salt."

"Besides, none of this is verifiable. It makes an interesting story, but that's all it is. A story," Max said with a condescending smile.

I huffed. "Is there any way to see who Madeline's visitors are and have been in prison, John?"

"Easy enough for my hacker."

"What about any records on Elizabeth? Does the state ever release that kind of information to the public?"

He shrugged. "Hoss is not cheap. And Hessor is no longer a client. I don't see where this would—"

"Take it out of my pay."

John's eyes got hard. "Why?"

"Why what?"

"Why do you need to know this?"

"I'm curious."

"Mel, look at the trouble it got you in with Meddleson case because of your curiosity. Let it go." John's tone got hard.

Max sat up just a bit, his head swiveling from John to me and back. "What sort of trouble?"

I grimaced at John as we both ignored Max. "What harm could it cause? You don't lose any money, Hoss makes money, and I get to satisfy my curiosity."

"I'll think about it." John said. He sat up setting the police file on the desk. "Speaking of pay, did you ever finish those employee checks?"

I frowned. "Yesterday. They're on Rich's desk."

"What about the info on that skip trace I asked you about?"

"What, are you my boss or something? Not yet. I'll do it now." I headed out of the office. The door closed behind me. I stopped in the hallway and stared at it. *What are they doing in there?*

***

It was after five when Max returned to the office to get me. I'd let him take my jeep to do some 'errands.' He just sat in the chair when John leaned on the doorpost.

"Yes?" I asked John.

He smiled. "You focus on the strangest things: dogs, statues…"

I smiled too. "Hoss came through."

John nodded. "Madeline has a long list of visitors over the years, but I think the one that you were looking for was Martin Accard. According to records, he's visited her almost every month since her incarceration."

"Really?"

Max's eyebrows disappeared into his hair.

"Better. After two years, she applied and received conjugal visits from him."

"No way!" This got better and better all the time. The look on John's face was one I'd never seen before. "There's more, isn't there?"

"Elizabeth's records at Charles County Rehab were harder to find, but Hoss did. She indeed was impregnated by someone at the institution. A rape. Martin had only visited her twice in her one year there."

"He visits his wife only twice, but his sister-in-law every month?" Max asked. "Must have been some hanky-panky going on."

John chuckled. "Better still… Elizabeth's pregnancy…" He paused.

"Her first?"

"Bingo. She couldn't have been Hessor's mom."

My eyes caught Max's. He smirked.

"You got lucky," Max said.

John started chuckling. "Want to hear something even stranger?"

167

I perked up. "Yeah?"

"Hoss also got a hold of Madeline's health record from the prison."

"How?" Max asked.

"Hoss has ways," John said with a wink. "Madeline had stretch marks and had given birth."

"No way!"

John's smile was across his whole face. "Elizabeth was most noted for crying herself to sleep at the institution. The file on her states that she called out all the time for 'Horace.'"

"Oh this is soap opera time." I chuckled. "You don't think that Madeline was bopping her brother-in-law at the same time that Horace was bopping his sister-in-law?"

Both men chuckled.

"That would mean that Madeline could be Bart's real mom, not his Aunt."

"Yep," John said.

"This is too much. So Madeline gets pregnant by Martin. Horace finds out, they argue or something, she kills him. Martin had her eventually kill Elizabeth who was doing Horace before he died." I smiled. "Oh what a tangled web we weave."

"It doesn't matter," Max said breaking into my ramblings.

"Why?" I asked him seriously. "We have not only discovered Bart's real parents, but we've solved two murders. I call that a pretty good day."

"The evidence is circumstantial. The information from this Hoss guy is not admissible in court, mostly likely gotten illegally. Both murders are so cold, I doubt that we could get the statue from Hessor. And even if it still had blood on it, we wouldn't be able to verify it was Horace's. The case in St. Louis is not a murder, but an accident. They will not reopen it on such flimsy evidence, if it even was evidence. Neither Madeline nor Martin will talk, I guarantee, so there is no case at all."

I made a face. "Do you have to be a kill-joy?"

Max gave me a smile. "I'm just pointing out the obvious."

"It was a very good piece of deductive reasoning though. Good job," John said. "I'll call Hessor with the information anyway. He has the right to know our suspicions about his real parents." He pushed off the door frame and headed back to his office.

I sat back, satisfied at how my thoughts had proven right, even if we could do nothing with it. I heard Max chuckling. "What?"

"You are something, Tiger. Are you ready to go home?"

"Yeah." I shut down the computer. "I'm getting hungry."

"Good. Your appetite is coming back."

"Sort of."

"Where do you want to go and celebrate?"

"Celebrate?"

"You solved the case, more or less, even if we can't do anything about it." Max was already waiting for me at the door. "I think that deserves a reward. I'm buying."

"Okay." I stood up as I rearranged some files on my desk for the next day. "By the way, what have you and John been cooking up?"

"Nothing."

"Nothing?"

"Now if I told you, it would spoil the surprise." Max put his hand on the small of my back and pushed me toward the front door.

"We're out of here, John," I called over my shoulder as Max patted my butt.

"Then it's home to celebrate." He raised his eyebrows in a sexy way.

I got all tingly and warm. Yes, it would be a good night tonight.

***

I was cuddled up with Max later in bed when a thought struck me. I jerked just a bit in surprise, causing Max to awaken.

"What?" he asked sleepily.

"Virginia Nefort."

"Yeah."

"I think I know... Beth said on the answering machine that she couldn't get the girl's name that Brady was seeing, but she was pretty sure that she was still in the area."

"I'm lost," Max admitted. "Again, please."

169

"Virginia Nefort. What if the lady living at the farm is Virginia Nefort's daughter. I seem to recall… I wonder…" I got up and headed to the third bedroom that I had converted to an office of sorts. I popped on my laptop and started surfing.

Max slowly followed me, rubbing his eyes. His shorts were once more hanging on his hips. And his cut chest was very sexy in the soft light of the hall. He leaned on the post. "It's after midnight. Are you sleeping tonight at all?"

"Yeah, in a minute. I think…" I stopped surfing and read the information. "Bingo."

"What?" he asked moving into the room heading to my side.

"Trisha Bashington, the renter at the farm was married. Her maiden name was Nefort."

Max read over my shoulder. "And you think Brady is living with her?"

"Yeah, maybe. I mean I saw the scuff marks in the room at the old house. What if he had chained Carmine there and would visit occasionally and feed her and stuff? It's possible."

Max slowly nodded his head. "Yeah. It is." He rubbed his chin. "There's one way to find out."

"How?"

"Let's go do some surveillance on Bashington's farm house." He smiled. "Maybe you'll be lucky again and we'll catch Brady."

With a smile I followed him out of the room.

Chapter 11

Even with bug spray, the mosquitoes were annoying. I felt like I was an all you can eat buffet. We were sitting in the woods right off of the farm house, surrounded by trees, watching the place. We could see Trisha's car parked by the house.

It was an older run down house, two stories, with a front and back entrance. Lots of windows but no lights.

Max had taken a quick tour around the place checking it out, but either no one was home or she was in bed. There was a soft light, possibly a night light, in one room upstairs, but other than that it looked deserted.

After looking around the house, he had also checked out the barn sitting only fifty feet from the main house. It was a two story barn, used in older days when the farm was actually worked. The hay loft had two doors opening from it, one in front, the other facing the concrete silo that had been used to store grain at one point. It was as tall as the barn but had no roof.

Max said the barn was deserted. I had hoped he would have found Brady's truck in there, but it was empty. The only thing in the barn was a lot of brush and other trash, probably collected from the years of disuse.

So now we sat. Waiting. Watching.

"Why don't you lean against me and take a nap," Max whispered. "I'll wake you in two hours, and then you can do the same for me."

I hesitated but agreed. I was tired and achy. I hadn't been achy since I had started the new drugs. With a silent nod, I got comfortable and snuggled in tight. It was hot, but he was comfortable. I fell asleep to him gently stroking my arm.

***

I was getting ready to wake Max for his next shift when a soft, almost unheard noise got my attention. My eyes immediately sprang to the back of the house, as much of it as we could see. There was that noise again. Someone was moving on the back porch.

I nudged Max awake with a finger to his lips. He came instantly awake and alert. I pointed to the back of the house.

The night was just starting to think about giving way to dawn, but the clouds that had gathered still kept the dark in play. We could definitely make out someone working on the back porch.

"Any lights?" Max whispered.

I shook my head. "Too big for Trisha."

"Yeah." Max's eyes fled up and down the yard checking things out.

The man stepped off the porch and headed to the barn. He was carrying something in his hand. It almost looked like a pot or dish.

I glanced at Max who grimaced.

"Call Rich or John. Get someone here now. I'm heading toward the barn from that direction. Stay here," Max said and silently took off, staying in the shadows of the trees.I grabbed my cell off my belt and dialed John's number.

"'Lo." John had been asleep.

"John," I whispered.

"Why are you whispering?"

"Max and I are at the farm house. We see Brady. He's taking what looks like something to eat to the barn. Get someone out here fast."

"On our way. Be careful."

I closed the phone and headed in the opposite direction from Max, but also toward the barn. By the time I arrived at the front barn door, I could hear Carson speaking. It sounded like he was above me in the loft.

"Eat faster. I need to head back to my camp in the woods."

"I'm thirsty, Daddy."

"Shut up. You'll drink when you're done eating. Or are you done now?"

"No." The word was said with food in her mouth.

I grimaced. The poor girl. I heard movement coming my way from the other side of the barn and saw Max moving toward me.

When he spotted me, he screwed up his face in anger.

I smiled. Even calling John, I had beaten him to the door. I pointed up and mouthed, 'Carmine.'

Max glanced around as he nodded.

I tapped him on the shoulder and mouthed, 'What to do?'

Max paused looking around again. I had no idea what he was looking for, but I could tell he was thinking hard. He pivoted around looking behind him and at the house.

I followed his gaze then moved to his side. We were on one side of the old double door to the barn. I turned quickly back to the barn as scraping noises were heard from above us. As I did, I doubled over in pain.

Max grabbed me and pulled me down to a squat against the side of the barn. He moved in front of me.

Brady's voice sounded above us. "Good. Now hand me the water bottle back. I'll be back tonight and then we're leaving here. Trisha and I are heading to Montana. If you remain silent and don't make any noise, we'll take you with us. Otherwise, I'll leave you here and you can starve to death."

"Please, Daddy. I'll be good. I'll be silent. I promise. I didn't even make a noise when some animal was in the barn earlier."

Max's head came back from his glance up with a grimace. He pushed me harder to the ground, his grip tightening on my arms. He moved inches from my face. 'Stay put,' he mouthed.

I made a face at him as I rubbed my side.

He let go of me and pointed right in my face. 'Stay.' He moved into the barn.

I grimaced in pain again but stayed leaning on the barn. I knew that I was more of a liability to him right now than an asset. Besides, someone had to let the cops know where Carmine was. My ears were straining to hear anything.

173

Footsteps sounded from across the loft. Then I heard a pause in his steps. Finally I could hear him moving down what sounded like a ladder.

The next thing I heard was a scuffle, grunts and crashing.

"Give it up Carson, the police are on their way," Max said right before another crash.

"No one is taking me alive. And my daughter belongs to me." Another crash. "I'll kill her before I let her go back to that bitch."

Max grunted loudly then another crash.

I peeked around the corner of the door, but I couldn't make out much. I heard something crash into the wall and the sound of glass breaking. A soft puff sounded. At the same time, I saw a body come flying toward me, moving fast.

I heard Max's muffled cursing from the far side of the barn as Brady passed me in the door. I extended my foot and tripped him.

We both stood up at the same time.

"Bitch," he yelled at me as he swung.

My hand went up automatically from my Judo training and deflected the majority of the punch, but his fist caught the side of my face. I went down hard on my side. Pain spiked through my chest. Again.

I heard running as a body sped by me.

"Get him," I grunted in pain.

Max hesitated just a second then took off running. Their footfalls faded quickly.

I sat up and rubbed my chin. That hurt. And the pain in my chest was not going away. I glanced in the direction the men were running, but they were already too far away for me to see. Slowly I picked myself off the ground.

Flickering light coming from the barn caught my attention. I moved to the door to see that the soft puff that I had heard was some sort of ignition. Part of the barn was on fire. And it was spreading fast.

I hesitated. My mind flashed to the doctor's office. 'No smoky environments. If you stress your lungs, it could lead to a collapse of your system. No chemical inhalants. Do not be around sick people. Your system is compromised. Any bug might send you down a spiral that you might not recover from. We are talking about your life here,

Ms. Addison. You've been lucky so far. Take these precautions and you should be able to live a normal life.'

I shook my head looking toward the loft. I glanced around the yard hoping to see rescue help for Carmine. But the fire was spreading fast, and I knew I was her only hope. Not only was this a fire, but God only knew what sort of chemicals had been stored in here or were still being stored in here.

I heard a muffled cry above me.

Without another thought, I headed directly to the ladder stairs in the middle, and even as I felt the heat from the fire, I climbed the steps.

By the time I reached the top, smoke was starting to fill the barn. It was hard to see even with the light the fire was providing. My lungs were fighting for breath already. It was hot and smoky. Coughing, I tried to find the girl.

"Carmine!"

No answer.

"Carmine, please. I need to find you." More coughing. "Your mom wants you back."

Suddenly I heard a whimper and crying off to the side. "Here."

I followed the sound as it was now very hard to see. "Where?" I asked around my coughing.

Carmine was coughing too. "Here. Over here."

I quickly moved toward her voice and found her desperately trying to untie a rope around her ankle. I squatted down and patted her hands away.

The knots were tight and had apparently been that way for a while because they wouldn't budge. I was coughing more and more now. My lungs were burning.

Carmine was coughing and crying. She was tugging at the rope.

"Stop moving. I can't get…" I stopped working on the knots, we didn't have time. I stood up and looked around as best I could. I batted the smoke from around me trying to find something, anything, to cut the rope.

I could hear the barn burning under us. The sound of crackling was growing louder and louder. One side of the barn sounded like it was getting ready to collapse. My eyes flicked around the area, desperate.

I followed the length of rope to where it was tied to the barn on the other side of the loft. The fire was already burning that wall. My head swiveled to our side of the loft. The door that opened toward the silo was on this side.

I could feel the air getting hotter by the second. A breeze had begun to blow the hot air around. I knew we didn't have much longer.

I squatted by Carmine and looked her in the eyes.

She was scared beyond belief. Her eyes were smudged with dirt and her nose was running with green snot. She had been sick recently.

I grabbed her by the shoulders. "We have one…" Cough. "Shot at this." Cough. Now I was coughing almost continually.

She just stared with wide brown eyes.

"Watch that wall. The fire should burn through the rope soon. We'll leave through that door."

Carmine shook her head. "It goes straight down."

"It's only one floor, about ten feet. Anything is better than burning," I yelled, moving to the door. "Watch that rope." I tried to open the door, but it was stuck. I took a step back and put my foot into it. It budged a bit.

"It's burning!"

"Pull on the rope!" I yelled back. The noise of the fire was almost louder than our yells. I took another deep, pain-searing breath and kicked at the mechanism holding the door closed. It burst open. I fell to the floor in agony. My lungs felt like they were on fire and only half inflated.

I stumbled back to the girl's side to find her tugging desperately on the rope. Although the wall was burning, the rope still held tight to the beam. I gave a tug but it wouldn't move.

Holding onto the rope, I tugged as I hurried to the beam. It was burning, just not as fast as the wall itself. The heat was terrible on this side of the loft.

My right arm was tucked tight against my chest, my left hand was over my mouth and nose trying to protect my lungs from the scorching heat. I kicked at the knot holding the rope tight. On the third kick it came free. I grabbed the end and scrambled back even as I felt the floor creaking around me.

Somehow I made it back to Carmine. She was sobbing uncontrollably. I grabbed her and shook her hard. "Stay with me Carmine." I literally dragged her to the open door.

It was a shade cooler near the door, and I could feel the colder air rushing past us as it fed the fire behind and under us. The floor shifted. I knew it would collapse soon.

I looked down and vertigo hit hard. Swirling. Pulsating. Stomach clenching fear. I froze.

"MEL!"

My eyes flew to the sound. It was directly across from me. I saw Max on top of the silo across from us. I opened my mouth, but I only coughed.

Max turned and pulled something up from behind him. It was a board. A narrow board. He pushed it toward me from the top of the silo. I grabbed it and laid it down on the edge of the sill. I looked down again. The ground seemed even farther away.

"Come on! You don't have time," Max yelled above the noise of the fire.

I hesitated just once, but pulled Carmine next to me. I gathered up the rope still attached to her leg and handed it to her. "Go to Max." I pointed across the short distance.

She shook her head and wouldn't go. Here pupils were so wide it looked like she had black eyes.

"Take my hand." I coughed and pushed her onto the board. I glanced over to see Max leaning out over the edge as far as possible. His hand was also extended. "Go." I pushed her again.

She took a step, still looking at me. Her hand had a death grip on mine. Her eyes locked with mine, but she moved, inching her way across the board.

It dipped with her weight, but held. She was just at our arms length. I looked across to see that she could just reach Max's hand.

"Let go." I heard Max yell.

She glanced my way. Her gripped tightened even more. She froze. I tried releasing her hand, but her death grip was too tight.

"Let go!" Max yelled again.

177

Finally she did, and then she was literally pulled across the rest of the board. I watched as she disappeared behind Max. Now I looked at the board, then behind me at the fire licking at my back.

"MEL!"

I looked across the expanse, and it seemed to grow with each passing nanosecond. I looked down.

"Don't Look Down! Look at me."

I brought my eyes up to Max. He had one foot on the board and his hand extended as far as possible. His eyes were pleading with me.

Two sides of the barn starting collapsing.

"NOW!" Max stretched his hand to me again. "Come on Tiger."

I looked down and took a tentative step onto the board.

"Don't stop. Just walk. Look into my eyes."

I looked at him. I had trouble breathing, but I trusted him. With our eyes locked, I walked. I just put one foot in front of the other. I focused totally on his face.

"Faster!"

I moved faster and felt the board groaning under my weight. That scared me, and I hesitated just a fraction of a second. At that instant, I felt Max's hand dig into my wrist. I felt myself being yanked forward.

A pain shot through my chest and arm at the same time that the board gave way. I was flung onto something relatively soft. Then a bear hug.

"Mel... Mel... breath Mel... Oh God!"

The whole world was shaking. I blinked and saw Max staring at me.

"Breathe!"

I did but it hurt. God, did it hurt. My lungs were on fire. I started coughing. And I was picked up, being carried somewhere. All I could do was cough.

"Down the ladder, Carmine. Be careful of the metal. Go on. Move it."

I felt movement, but all I could really feel was pain. My chest, my lungs, my throat, my back was hurting like hell. It seemed to feel better if I closed my eyes. So I did and laid my head on Max's shoulder.

The next thing I knew I was laid down in coldness. It was cold around me compared to the heat from the fire. I looked around still coughing.

Carmine was sitting next to me on the grass, coughing and crying. She was huddled in a ball, holding her chest and gasping for air.

A hand brushed hair away from my eyes. I looked straight up to see Max smiling.

"Keep breathing, but slow down. I know it hurts, Tiger. You are safe." He leaned down and kissed me on the forehead. "Sirens are approaching."

I tried to ask about Brady, but all I could do was cough. As I sucked in air, I could hear myself wheezing. I watched as Max reached out to Carmine, then pulled her into a hug.

"I know you're scared Carmine. It's okay. The police are almost here. You're safe. Breathe, Mel. You need to keep breathing. I'll get you help as soon as possible. You did good, Tiger. Slow your breathing."

"Can't... breathe."

Max's eyes got a worried look even as he smiled. "Help is on the way. Slow breathing."

I tried a smile, but the pain was too much. I closed my eyes. I felt Max pat my shoulder. I heard Max talking with Carmine, but not much of it registered. I think Max was talking on his phone too. And sirens, I heard sirens in the distance.

The next thing I remember was Max's urgent voice. "She needs help now. We can't wait." I was picked up—Max's strong arms. Within seconds I was transferred to other arms. Then I was handed back to Max. I was on his lap in the back of a squad car. I looked up to see John looking in at us. He winked at me then we took off.

"Easy, Mel. Deeper breaths, slow your breathing. You are breathing way too fast. Slow it down. We're meeting the ambulance on the way." Max hugged me.

"Car... Carmine?" I managed to wheeze out around a cough.

"In the front seat. She's fine." Max leaned down and kissed me on the cheek. "Just keep breathing. Don't give up."

"So the girl here was kidnapped by her father?" I heard the cop driving ask.

"Yeah," Max answered him. "Her name is Carmine Carson. Her mom lives in New Jersey. When we get to the hospital, I'll call Rich Addison and he can give you the particulars." Max paused. "Carmine, would you like to talk to your Mom?"

A sob and coughing came from the front seat. "Yeah."

"As soon as the doctors check you out, Carmine," the officer driving said.

It wasn't much longer and the car was slowing down.

Max looked me in the eyes. "The ambulance is here, Tiger."

I was man-handled out of the back of the squad car and put on a gurney. Quickly I was placed in the ambulance. Oxygen was placed on my face, but it didn't seem to be helping much. I still struggled for a breath.

A paramedic's face appeared above me. "Mel, we need to intubate you, put a tube down your throat to help you breathe. I think that your throat may have been burned."

I stared up. He looked familiar.

"Yes, you know me. I was a year behind you in school. Brent Garrett."

Sure.

"Don't fight me with the tube. It will be uncomfortable for a few seconds, but it will help you breathe. Okay?"

I nodded still wheezing.

He moved to be at the top of my head.

I opened my mouth. I'd had a tube in me before. I felt the instrument in my throat, then the familiar choking feeling of the tube in me. After a couple seconds, at which I tried not to jump off the gurney, it eased, and I could breathe a little better.

"All done." Bret smiled as he taped the tube to my face. "Deep breaths. That should help."

Indeed it did, and I didn't feel like I was suffocating anymore. I relaxed a bit. I was left alone for just a second, and I saw the other paramedic working on Carmine. She had oxygen on, and the guy was asking her questions.

I could hear Brent talking on the radio to someone. I looked back at Carmine and she smiled. She glanced at the paramedic and took off the oxygen for a second.

"Thanks." Then she put it back on.

I nodded at her and tried to smile. The tube made it hard though.

Brent looked down after he inserted an IV in my arm. "We're heading to the hospital now." He continued to work on me.

I nodded and saw Max scoot onto the bench seat in the back of the ambulance. He smiled as the ambulance began to move and grabbed my hand.

"Feeling better?"

I nodded just a bit and closed my eyes. It still hurt, but at least I wasn't gasping anymore. I think I fell asleep or passed out because I heard Max answering questions, then I remember nothing.

Chapter 12

I awoke with a jump. My throat felt raw, and I tried swallowing but couldn't. *What's going on? Where am I?*

Actually opening my eyes, I saw that I was in a hospital. And from the machines around me, I must be in intensive care. I moved slightly to see my heart being monitored and two other machines that I didn't recognize. *What happened?*

In the next instant I remembered the burning barn and Carmine. I lifted my hand and looked at it. It was tingling. And it was a shade of red. The other hand was the same.

A nurse appeared over my head. "Good morning, Ms. Addison. You have a tube in your throat, so you can't talk." She smiled. "It's just a precaution, and the doctor says it might come out soon. You're in intensive care for a day or so, just to make sure that you'll be okay." She looked toward a machine.

I glanced with her.

When she looked back down she still had a smile on her face. "Are you in an excessive amount of pain?"

I shook my head no. Then I pointed at the red tint to my hand.

She nodded. "Your hands and a small part of your back has first and second degree burns. Your face too. They did a bronchoscope on you. Your throat also is slightly burnt, but the lungs are not burned. From what we've been told by your boyfriend, the smoke has probably irritated a previous condition in your lungs. Is that right?"

I nodded.

"So, we're being extra careful. Dr. Corbet will be in shortly." She glanced at her watch. "I can allow visitors for a few minutes. Do you feel up to it?"

I tried a smile with a nod.

She disappeared from my side.

Shortly Mom and Dad appeared next to me. I could tell from their eyes they were very worried but tried not to let me know. I sighed. *Not again! Where is Max?*

Dad gave out a chuckle. "Max said we should come in first."

I smiled back and squeezed his hand. Mom had a hold of my other hand. I looked at Dad then pointed out the door. At his puzzled look, I motioned to write.

He quickly produced a slip of paper and pen. He held the paper and put the pen in my hand.

'Carmine?' I wrote.

"She's fine. She's being kept in the hospital too for observation. But her mom arrived early this morning." Dad patted my shoulder. "I'm proud of you, Sweetie."

'Brady Carson?'

Dad's smile reached epic proportions. "Max caught him. Knocked him out. He was still unconscious when the State Police arrived. He's in custody."

'Time?' I noticed that it was light out. Maybe afternoon.

"It's three in the afternoon," Mom answered. "You had us worried there for awhile. "Do you remember waking up in the emergency room?"

I shook my head.

"That's okay. They gave you drugs to make you sleep so you wouldn't stress your throat." She kissed me on the cheek. "But not to worry. Someone will be here when you wake up from now on."

I smiled at her. Although that smothered feeling was creeping up again, it felt nice right now. I looked at Dad as my eyes dipped. I was immensely tired.

"Go to sleep, Mel," Mom said softly. She leaned over and kissed me again, this time on the forehead. "We all love you."

Yep. It was starting again. I let myself slip into the welcome sleep. No tube in my throat was going to help this feeling of being smothered.

***

Three days later I was still in the hospital. The tube had been taken out the day before. Twelve hours after the fire, my throat had almost completely closed up due to swelling from the heat and tissue damage.

Dr. Corbet wanted me in the hospital another three days. He had consulted with Dr. Changri in Maryland and in order to run the tests that I needed as often as I needed them, I should stay. So, I was stuck.

Now I was bored. The TV was off because there was nothing to watch. Mom had been up earlier in the morning and afternoon. Now it was after supper, and I wanted company but not enough to call around and ask someone to come and visit. That would have left a flood gate open for visitors.

I was worried though. I hadn't seen Max since the night before. He had left with a mysterious, 'I'll be back tomorrow.'

Rich had stopped by in the afternoon briefly to give me news about Carmine and her family. They were back in New Jersey. Happy. Carson was in jail and denied bail, waiting extradition to New Jersey for his nefarious deeds. And… his grin grew bigger. "John told Hessor about what you discovered. Apparently, Hessor doesn't get along with Martin Accard. And was even angrier that his mom had been seeing Accard regularly in jail. He said he's going to confront Madeline next time he visits her. John said he was extremely pissed off."

When I asked about John, Rich shrugged. "Haven't seen him since last night. He and Max met up after visiting hours last night."

I thought about our conversation again and frowned. *What were the two of them cooking up? And why were they being so secretive?*

The door slowly swung open. It wasn't a nurse; just someone barging in. The person was backing into the room and carrying a bouquet of flowers. I knew that body. It was Max.

"Where have you been?" I asked in my hoarse voice. My vocal cords were still healing.

"Busy," Max said, busy putting the flowers on the table. He was at an angle so I couldn't see his face.

I focused on the roses and baby's breath and other flowers I couldn't identify. "Why the flowers?" My eyes moved to Max, but I still couldn't see his face.

"To ward off your temper." He turned. Max had a black eye, and the left side of his chin was swollen. If he didn't have a beard, I bet I would see that it was badly bruised.

"What happened?"

Max smiled. Under his arm he carried a newspaper. He sat on the side of my bed before answering. "How are you?"

"Stop evading my questions."

He handed me the paper.

I unfolded it to see that it was today's edition of the Quincy Herald Whig, the local newspaper. I glanced at him.

He pointed to the paper.

I focused on the headlines.

"Local man arrested in St. Louis for drugs." I glanced again at Max, but when he just smiled, I turned my attention back to the paper. It continued, "A local man was arrested in St. Louis on charges that range from drug possession, intent to sell, and assault and battery. Bartholomew Hessor was arrested outside of the dance club, Rascals, in St. Louis early this morning with ten grams of cocaine on his person after the police were called to break up a fight. When police arrived, Mr. Hessor was beating a man up, and the police took him into custody. The other man is unidentified. Mr. Hessor was arrested and is being held in Charles County Correctional Center pending a bail hearing next week."

I looked up at Max and studied his face. "Unidentified?"

"Money works wonders."

"You let him beat you up?"

Max shook his head. "He looks just as bad. Worse. I stopped fighting when the police arrived. I know how to work the system." He winked with his black eye, grimacing in pain.

"Bart is too smart to carry drugs on him."

Max shrugged.

I narrowed my eyes. "You've been planning this with John, haven't you?"

"Not me. I went down there to tell him to leave you alone." Max paused. "It got out of hand."

"I see." I crossed my arms. He was a horrible liar.

Max just stared at me. "Are you mad at me?"

"For getting Bart arrested?"

Max nodded.

"Why should I? He's a boil on the back end of society." My arms were still crossed in anger.

"Then why?"

I didn't answer.

"The fight?"

I still didn't answer. To be honest, I wasn't quite sure myself why I was mad. But I certainly wasn't going to tell him that.

Max shifted under my gaze. Then he suddenly smiled. "At least I didn't break his nose." He tapped me on my nose. "You should see Phillip. He's already arranging for plastic surgery."

My eyes widened just a bit.

"Oh, I know all about it." Max leaned down and kissed me. "Fighting for my honor." He kissed me again. "Gotta love a woman that fights for her man."

"You aren't 'my man.'"

"Sure, Mel." He winked at me with his good eye. "I love you anyway."

I merely huffed at him as he started laughing.